THE FIRST LAST DAY

THE FIRST LAST DAY

D O R I A N
C I R R O N E

Aladdin
NEW YORK LONDON TORONTO SYDNEY NEW DELHI

ALADDIN
An imprint of Simon & Schuster Children's Publishing Division
1230 Avenue of the Americas, New York, New York 10020
First Aladdin hardcover edition June 2016

For information about special discounts for bulk purchases, please contact
Simon & Schuster Special Sales at 1-866-506-1949 or
business@simonandschuster.com.
The Simon & Schuster Speakers Bureau can bring authors to your live event.
For more information or to book an event contact
the Simon & Schuster Speakers Bureau at 1-866-248-3049
or visit our website at www.simonspeakers.com.
Jacket designed by Laura Lyn DiSiena
Interior designed by Hilary Zarycky
The text of this book was set in Scala.
Manufactured in the United States of America 0516 FFG
2 4 6 8 10 9 7 5 3 1
Library of Congress Cataloging-in-Publication Data
Names: Cirrone, Dorian, author.
Title: The first last day / by Dorian Cirrone.
Description: First Aladdin hardcover edition. | New York : Aladdin, 2016. |
Summary: Eleven-year-old Haleigh Adams paints a picture with a mysterious set of paints found in her backpack and now she is stuck in a time loop, but when she realizes her parents have been keeping a secret she and her new best friend Kevin must find the source of the magic paints and the secret of the time loop before it is too late.
Identifiers: LCCN 2015028695 | ISBN 9781481458139 (hc) | ISBN 9781481458153 (eBook)
Subjects: | CYAC: Time—Fiction. | Magic—Fiction. | Friendship—Fiction. | Secrets—Fiction. | BISAC: JUVENILE FICTION / Social Issues / Friendship. | JUVENILE FICTION / Family / Multigenerational. | JUVENILE FICTION / Fantasy & Magic.
Classification: LCC PZ7.C499 Fi 2016 | DDC [Fic]—dc23
LC record available at http://lccn.loc.gov/2015028695

In memory of four women, much like G-Mags,
who enriched my life in so many ways:

Karen "Buffey" Barisano
Frances Bertuccio
Susan Giannini
Mary Koncsol

Life can only be understood backward,

but it must be lived forward.

—Søren Kierkegaard

CHAPTER 1

I once read that the Eiffel Tower can grow more than six inches in summer because heat makes iron expand.

When I said that to Kevin, he stopped on the boardwalk and turned to me wide-eyed, like I'd just revealed the secret plot to the next *Star Wars* movie. "Do you know what that means?" he asked. "If people were made of iron, you'd be five feet three—and I'd be five feet ten."

I straightened my back and stretched my neck. "In a really hot summer, maybe even taller." As I let myself imagine that I wasn't always the shortest twelve-year-old in the room, Kevin took his notebook out of his backpack and jotted something down. "What are you writing?" I asked.

"An idea for a movie: a kid who becomes a giant every summer but shrinks back to normal size when it's over."

"Interesting. But who would you get to play the giant kid?"

As families strolled past us with dripping frozen custard cones and funnel cakes, Kevin thought for a minute. "I have a friend who's really tall. Maybe he—"

A *ping* sounded from Kevin's cell phone, and he stopped to read the text. "It's my mom. She and Dad just drove in from Montclair to take me home tomorrow."

"*Please,*" I begged. "Don't say that word."

"Which one? I said sixteen of them."

"'Tomorrow.' I'm trying to forget this is our last day at the shore."

Kevin's eyes gleamed as he put his phone away. "I've got something that'll cheer you up. Wait here."

"What is it?"

"A surprise," he said, taking off toward his grandmother's house.

Knowing Kevin, I figured it could be anything from a vintage Batman comic to a moldy potato chip that looked like Spider-Man. Neither of those would cheer me up.

The only thing I wanted that day was for summer not to end and for Kevin and me to stay friends after we left the shore.

While I waited, the familiar sound of squawking seagulls and the smell of coconut sunscreen drifting by on a warm breeze were comforting. The sameness of summer always made me feel safe and happy.

As soon as we left the shore, my dad was starting a new job at a big university, and we were moving to a new house. Again.

That meant another new school. And another year of making new friends. We'd moved four times already, and each time I thought I'd found a BFF, things would change once we weren't at the same school anymore. They'd be talking about things and people I didn't know, and before I knew it, they'd moved on. I hoped Kevin and I wouldn't drift apart like that when summer was over.

Even though we'd be at different schools, he didn't

live that far away from where we were moving. And I'd already figured out that if I left the next day at noon, he and I would have spent approximately seven hundred and twenty-four hours hanging out at the shore. That kind of time together had to mean something. It was more than I'd ever spent with anyone, except my parents. And maybe some random kid I'd sat next to in school because of our last names—like Tiffany Addison, who was always asking me why I drew people instead of cats. I love cats as well as the next person, but not when they're wearing tiaras and carrying purses, like the ones she drew all over her notebook. It was kind of demeaning to all catkind.

I tightened the band around my frizz of a ponytail and squinted toward the beach.

My mind's eye made an imaginary *click, click, click*:

Sunbathers lining the shore like stick figures.

Kids guarding their sand sculptures from the incoming tide.

And the endless line separating the periwinkle sky from the cerulean ocean.

I was about to take out my sketchpad to capture it all when I felt something behind me. Startled, I turned to find Kevin wearing a cow costume, complete with a hood that had pink ears sticking straight out to the sides—and an udder.

I eyed him up and down. "I see you've *beefed* up your wardrobe."

"Well done!" Kevin shot back. He spun in a circle. "What do you think, Hales?"

Kevin is the only person I'd ever let call me Hales. At the beginning of sixth grade, one girl started calling me Hale. Then some others gave me nicknames like Storm and Tornado. One kid even called me Acid Rain Adams. That was when I learned you have to be very careful when you let someone give you a nickname.

"What's up with the costume?"

"My mom saw one of those TV shows about hoarders, and now she's on a cleaning binge—it was in my closet back home. I couldn't let her give away something this cool."

"And . . . why did you have a cow costume in your closet?"

"Class project. Did you know a cow spends eight hours a day regurgitating and chewing her partially digested food?"

"Ew."

"And, one cow produces almost two hundred thousand glasses of milk in her lifetime?"

"Being a cow sounds tiring—and kind of gross."

"Being a fake cow is cool. I'll let you try on the costume."

"No thanks."

"C'mon," Kevin said. "I've only had it on for like fifteen minutes and I can already tell you something about everyone on the boardwalk."

Kevin's father is a psychologist, so Kevin thinks he can figure out everything about everybody. I pointed to a guy in beige shorts and a white T-shirt, licking a cherry Italian ice. "Okay, Dr. Cheeseburger, what's his story?"

"Let's see. He's very well adjusted and can cope with change. I know that because he looked at me, smiled, and went back to his Italian ice."

I motioned toward a woman wearing huge sunglasses and a white lace bathing suit cover-up. "What about her?" As the words came out of my mouth, she pressed her lips together and hurried by.

"That one has major anger issues," Kevin said.

"How can you know that? Maybe she's a vegetarian . . . or lactose intolerant."

"How could anyone look at me wearing this outfit and not smile? I look *udderly* ridiculous."

"You do look ridiculous."

"Ridiculously *fun*!" Kevin reached into his backpack and handed me his video camera to film him along the boardwalk. Then he shouted, "Lights, camera, action!"

I'd been helping Kevin with his science fiction movie all summer. He didn't know what it would be about, but he wanted to be ready with a lot of footage once he decided. I walked backward as I filmed. After several near collisions, I stopped and looked up at him. "What kind of science fiction movie would have a cow in it?"

Kevin thought for a second. "Vampire cows! It's got Oscar winner written all over it."

I gave him the camera and laughed. "More like Oscar Mayer."

"Good one," Kevin said, smiling.

The first time I saw that smile was when I bumped into him, literally, at the beginning of summer. Both of us stared straight up at the sky as we walked along the boardwalk. I was studying the exact shade of blue, for a painting, when our shoulders smacked each other hard. "Whoa," Kevin said. "Sorry."

"It's okay," I mumbled. Most kids would have kept going—but not Kevin.

"You know what I was wondering?" he asked.

Even though it was a weird question, the sparkle in his greenish brown eyes made me stop and ask, "What?"

"If you hung on a rope from a helicopter and hovered for about twelve hours while the Earth revolved, could you end up landing in a different country?"

I didn't know the answer. But once we started talking, I knew this kid would definitely take the bored out of the boardwalk for me. And I was right.

Kevin continued filming random people. Most sped by as soon as they saw him.

After a while I put my face close to the lens. "C'mon. We need to make the rest of this day special."

"Okay," Kevin said, stopping to think for a minute. "I know! G-Mags is making cannolis for tonight. Let's help her."

G-Mags was the nickname Kevin and his brother

gave their grandmother: *G* for Grandma and *Mags* for Margaret. She was a lot older than both my grandmothers, who live far away. I don't see them very often, but I had seen G-Mags almost every day over the summer.

"Sounds good to me," I said.

Kevin gave me that familiar grin. "Then let's get a *mooooove* on." Once we crossed the street, he kicked a rock and chased it toward his grandmother's house.

I watched as he and his cow suit grew smaller in the distance.

CHAPTER 2

While G-Mags deep-fried the cannoli shells, I stirred the two cheeses—ricotta and mascarpone—in a big bowl. Kevin added sugar, a few drops of vanilla, and some lemon zest. As I swirled the dark brown drops and yellow dots into the mixture, I painted a picture in my mind of the three of us: G-Mags peeking into her pot of oil and me pushing Kevin's hand away as he tried to dip his finger into the bowl. All of us were smiling.

The last time I'd helped cook anything was when we put our house up for sale. Mom and I made brownies almost every day. She said the smell would make buyers like our house better. She was right. We'd sold it just before coming to the shore.

"How are you doing with the filling?" G-Mags asked.

"Great," I said, looking up from the bowl.

G-Mags placed her tongs on a spoon rest in the shape of Kevin's hand. Her house was the complete opposite of the ones I'd lived in. She'd been there for so many years that everything Kevin and his brother, Michael, made for her was still on display: a picture of the two of them, framed in elbow macaroni, a ceramic cup with a hole that separates egg whites from the yolks, and my favorite, a portrait of Kevin that Michael had painted a long time ago. I hadn't met Michael because he was working in New York City for the summer. But as I looked around the house, I felt like I knew him.

"All done," I said as I handed Kevin the spoon to lick.

"Okay, you two," G-Mags said. "I have to let these shells cool. You can go have fun."

"What?" Kevin said. "You mean I can't eat one now?"

G-Mags gave him a hug. "We'll have them after dinner."

Kevin frowned and turned to me. “Hey, I almost forgot. Do you want to go to Atlantic City with my mom and dad? We’re leaving when they get back from the store.”

“Okay.” I wasn’t sure what we’d do in Atlantic City, but there was no way I was missing my last afternoon with Kevin. Just in case things turned out like they had with my last best friend, Abbey.

We’d been friends all through sixth grade. But toward the end of the year, Abbey got into wearing makeup and reading stuff on the Internet about fashion and famous people. I tried to act interested. One day when we were in the girls’ bathroom, she asked me for an opinion on her new lip gloss. “It’s nice,” I said.

She shook her head at me. “You really don’t care about my new lip gloss, do you?” Rolling her eyes, she turned toward a seventh grader, who was putting on mascara, and asked for a second opinion.

I’d e-mailed and texted her a few times after she left for camp but never got any answer. I figured she’d moved on—like everyone else.

CHAPTER 3

A rock I'd found on the boardwalk flew from my pocket when I tossed my shorts on the bed. I picked it up and traced the outline of a fish skeleton with my fingernail. This one was a beauty—definitely worthy of a drawing. I knew Mom would never let me keep all twenty-six fossils I'd collected, so I'd gotten into the habit of sketching them—along with everything else I couldn't keep. No matter how many times we moved, it was never easy to leave so many things behind.

After showering and throwing on a pair of shorts

and my new DON'T WORRY, I'M AN ARTIST T-shirt that Mom bought me, I headed to the living room to show her. Dad was working at his desk. "Where's Mom?"

"Last time I checked, she went to take a nap," he said without looking up.

Mom never used to sleep in the daytime, but suddenly she was napping every day. She said it was because of the heat.

"How's the research going?" I asked.

"Great," Dad answered, changing to his Professor Adams voice. "This article on Einstein is fascinating. Did you know—"

Before he could finish, Mom burst in from the porch. "What do you think?" she asked, holding a box filled with three small clay pots. "Will these be okay on the ride home?"

I glanced at the carton. "I thought you were sleeping."

"I almost forgot about these seeds G-Mags gave me. She said if I plant them now, I'll have a garden of herbs by the fall."

Mom had been acting weird all summer. One minute she forgot things and the next she acted like she was on some deadline. She put the box down. "Did I hear that you and Kevin have a date to go to Atlantic City?"

"It's not a date!" I said, louder than I wanted to. "The Damicos are here to take Kevin home tomorrow. The four of us are going to Atlantic City." Did Mom think I *liked* Kevin? The way Abbey told me she *like* liked that eighth grader who rapped at the school talent show?

Did I?

"I didn't mean that kind of date," Mom said.

I felt my face flush as a horn blasted from the driveway.

Mom reached for the fruit bowl on the counter. "You should take a healthy snack with you," she said, tossing a shiny, red apple my way.

It hit my hand and fell to the floor. I grabbed the apple and threw it back to her. All summer long, she'd been obsessed with eating healthy snacks. It wasn't like she used to let me eat Cheez Doodles and M&M's all the time. But she'd suddenly gone all health foodie. The week before, she'd tried to make Dad and me eat chips made out of some dark green leaves. (I wouldn't recommend them.)

I patted my backpack and told Mom I had enough money for food.

"Be careful," Dad said as I raced toward the door.

"And save some of that energy for packing," Mom added. "I'll need your help."

"Okay," I yelled back. But I couldn't help wondering what was up with Mom. Since when did she need my help doing anything?

CHAPTER 4

"Promise me you'll text every half hour," Mrs. Damico said as we stood in the middle of the hotel lobby. "And don't go outside." She's a behavior specialist in middle school, so she's really good at rule making. Once she finished her list of dos and don'ts, she took off with Kevin's dad toward the casino.

To our left, people sat on stools in front of slot machines, hypnotized. Kevin pulled out his camera. Immediately, a stern-faced security guard barked, "No filming!"

Kevin shoved the camera into his backpack. "That footage would have been perfect."

"For what?"

"*Vampire Cows Versus Zombies.* Genius, huh?"

I was about to agree when I spotted a woman in flowered pants walking up to an empty slot machine. She pulled a lever and, suddenly, bells and lights went off. "Look at that," I said. "She won on her first try."

"It's probably her first try at *that* machine," Kevin said. "G-Mags says most people put more money into the casino than they'll ever take out of it."

"Then why do they do it?"

"I guess it's fun, but it sure seems boring to me." Kevin pointed to a giant neon taco. "Hey, that place looks good." He pulled out his camera to get a quick shot of the neon sign.

"Don't tell me," I said. *"Attack of the Killer Tacos."*

Kevin tucked the camera back into his bag. "It's like you're reading my mind."

A few minutes later, we were seated at a table, looking at pictures of burritos and beans with melted cheese. "Can you believe this is our last dinner together?" I asked.

"It's only three thirty," Kevin said. "G-Mags is making ragout tonight. You're invited."

"It's not about the food. It's . . ."

Before I could finish, Kevin had peeled the paper end off his straw and stuck the plastic in his mouth. He blew the wrapper across the table, missing me by a couple of inches. I turned just in time to see the man behind me as he twisted to find out what hit him.

With his black hair, pale skin, and dark suit, the guy looked like he'd never been out in the sun. I leaned toward Kevin and whispered, "He could play a vampire in your movie."

Kevin grinned as our server approached us. Her long blond hair hung in curls, and her lips were flamingo pink.

I ordered tacos, and Kevin asked for a chicken quesadilla. When the waitress left, I eased into another conversation about staying in touch after summer. I may have been shorter and younger than a lot of seventh graders, but I knew enough not to come right out and ask someone if they'd always be your friend. That definitely would have bought me a seat on the train to Nerd Town.

I took a deep breath and chose my words carefully. "Don't you wish summer would never end?"

"It'll be tough to go back to school," Kevin said. "But it'll be great to start working on my movie. My mom and dad are getting me new computer software for my thirteenth birthday, and . . . I'll get to see Michael. How about you?" he asked. "You must be looking forward to something."

"I guess . . . private art classes with my new teacher. That'll be fun."

"You and Michael would really get along," Kevin said. "He's an amazing artist—just like you are. He's always painting or sketch—" Kevin stopped and got this weird look on his face, like he was confused or maybe mad about something.

"What is it?" I asked. "What did I do?"

"It's not you," he whispered. "It's that man behind you. He's been listening to our conversation. Now he's bending down toward the floor."

"Maybe he's still trying to figure out what hit him." I leaned over so I could find the straw paper before the man did, but Kevin shook his head and made a scary face. "Not yet," he mouthed.

Soon the scrape of the man's chair sounded from behind me. He glanced our way before passing us, swinging a large briefcase. "Maybe he's a writer," I whispered. "My mom says writers like to eavesdrop on people's conversations to get material for their novels."

Kevin got a familiar gleam in his eyes, the one he'd get when he thought of a joke or a pun. "He probably writes under the name I. M. Nosy."

I looked at the man again. "More like I. M. Creepy."

CHAPTER 5

C'mon, let's explore the hotel," Kevin said, heading toward a row of stores.

We looked in each of the shops, which all sold the same things: T-shirts, tiny glasses, mugs, and anything else big enough for the phrase I ♥ ATLANTIC CITY. In one store, Kevin picked up a box of saltwater taffy. "My treat," he offered.

I bared my braces at him. "Remember these. If I break a bracket, I lose my chance for a prize at the orthodontist."

"Right. Sorry. I forgot you have the diet of an

eighty-year-old. Maybe we can find you some souvenir soup or applesauce."

"Thanks a lot." I pivoted with pretend anger and left the shop. When I turned back to make sure Kevin was behind me, I spotted a familiar briefcase going around a corner. "Was that the writer again?"

"Maybe he's following us," Kevin said.

"Then why is he walking away?"

"Maybe that's how good spies follow people." Kevin rubbed his chin with exaggeration. "Very tricky."

I forgot about the man when a voice from a nearby shop sang out, "Voilà!" I gestured for Kevin to follow me toward a group gathered in front of Marty's Magic Shop. We were just in time to watch a guy, with a top hat and a black mustache curled up at the sides, pull a coin from behind an old man's ear.

Kevin wrinkled his brow. "You don't believe in magic, do you?"

"I know they're really tricks," I said. "But I can never figure them out. So, to me, it's magic."

"I guess."

A guy I assumed was Marty held up a deck of cards and asked a little girl to pick one. Her tiny fingers loosened a card wedged in the middle of the pack. She yanked it out, flattened it to her chest, and then peeked at it.

Marty instructed her to put it back into the deck. He shuffled the cards, held the pack in the air, and bellowed, "I will make the card that you picked rise from the pack." Slowly, the queen of hearts grew from the middle of the deck. "Was that your card?" Marty asked.

The girl's eyes widened as she nodded *yes*. The crowd gasped in amazement.

"He switched the cards," Kevin murmured. "I didn't see it, but I know he did."

"Thank you! Thank you!" Marty shouted as he took an exaggerated bow. "And now I have an even more mysterious trick: it's called the Vanishing Silk." He displayed his bare arms. "You see I have no sleeves in which to hide anything." He held up a red scarf with one hand and pointed to Kevin with the other. "You!" he shouted.

Everyone turned as Kevin put his finger to his chest and mouthed, "Me?"

"Yes, you seem doubtful," Marty said. "Do you

believe I can make this silk kerchief disappear?"

Kevin shrugged.

Marty turned back to the crowd and announced, "To the disbelievers like this young man here, I say . . . *Watch. Carefully.*"

Kevin whispered in my ear, "I wish there really was such a thing as magic, so I could make Marty disappear."

I bit my upper lip to keep from laughing as Marty made a fist with one hand and stuffed the scarf into it. Waving his free hand over the fist, he yelled, "Voilà!" In an instant, he opened both hands wide. The scarf was gone!

I elbowed Kevin. "How do you think he did that?"

Kevin's eyes became suspicious slits. "I don't know, but I know it's not magic."

All of a sudden, Marty headed toward me. The crowd parted. I froze.

He reached behind me, toward my backpack, and shouted, "Aha!" He flourished the scarf in the air and exclaimed, "*You* stole it!"

A wave of whispers made its way across the room.

A flush crept up my neck. How had he done that?

Marty looked at me with a twinkle in his eye. He used his free hand to twirl his mustache and then turned away, shouting, "All magic tricks are available for purchase!"

Kevin shook his head. "I still don't believe in magic."

CHAPTER 6

Okay," Kevin said. "We've eaten, watched people gamble, seen a magic show, and we still have more than an hour before we have to meet my parents. What should we do?"

"Hmm. Eating. Shopping. Gambling. That's about all there is."

"Wait a minute," Kevin said, pointing toward some glass doors. "A windmill! There's a miniature golf course across the boardwalk. Are you up for a game?"

"Sure."

"Stay here," he said. "My mom's not answering her

cell. I'll find her and ask if it's okay if we go outside."

While he was gone, I studied the people walking along the boardwalk. I was deep in thought when I felt my backpack being jostled. Startled, I turned to find Kevin with a big smile on his face. "Did I scare you?"

"No. What were you doing?"

"Your backpack was open. I was zipping it up."

"How did that happen?"

Kevin wiggled his fingers and made a spooky noise. "Maybe it was magic."

"I know there's no such thing as magic."

"Unless you count my amazing mini-golf skills."

"I'm sure."

"You doubt me? Well, get ready for some major mini-golf butt kicking!"

At the first hole, the Mad Hatter, the object was to get the ball into a large hat. Kevin got the ball in with one swing. It took me three. At the second hole, Jack and Jill, the ball had to go over a small hill. "Only three tries!" Kevin shouted. It took me six.

"Why is it so easy for you?"

Kevin leaned on his golf club and grinned. "Because I'm awesome?" I tried to kick the club out from

underneath him, but he jumped away. "You know I'm kidding," he said. "It's because I get more practice—with my friends at home."

After Kevin took only three shots to get the ball between the windmill's paddles, I took eight tries. "Can't I start over?" I asked, ignoring the group of kids behind me yelling for us to hurry up.

"You mean you want a mulligan?" Kevin asked.

"Huh?"

"That's what they call a do-over in golf," Kevin said. "My dad taught me."

"Then, yes, I want a mulligan." It took six swings that time.

When we finally reached the eighteenth hole, Kevin popped the ball in with one stroke. "Your turn," he said, examining the scorecard. "Let's see, if you get a hole in one, you'll only lose by thirty points."

I laughed and hit the ball. It fell into the hole like an exclamation point. I jumped up and down in victory.

"Not bad," Kevin said, smiling. He grabbed my club and headed toward the front counter while I stopped to fix my sandal strap. As I got up, a bicyclist pulling a rickshaw along the boardwalk rammed right into

Kevin's shoulder, hurling him to the ground. The driver kept on going.

I raced toward Kevin, who was sitting up and staring straight ahead. His knee was bleeding, and he was kind of scraped up but looked okay. "Should I get your mom?" I asked between frantic breaths.

He shook his head, tore off a corner of the scorecard, and stuck it on the cut.

I helped him up and reached for my backpack. That was when I realized I'd left it by the windmill. After making my way through the crowd of kids who had been playing behind us, I grabbed the bag and sprinted back to Kevin. "Whew, that was close," I said. "All my stuff is in here."

I hugged the backpack to my chest and checked Kevin's knee one more time before we headed inside the hotel.

CHAPTER 7

"*Klaatu barada nikto*," Kevin said as he stepped into the kitchen.

G-Mags looked up from the stove. Her forehead wrinkled above her gold-rimmed glasses. "Whatever are you talking about?"

"It's from the old black-and-white version of *The Day the Earth Stood Still*," Kevin said. "We just caught the last half on TV. When the robot hears those words, he brings his friend back to life. It's the best. Right, Hales?"

I nodded, even though I wasn't an expert on old sci-fi films like Kevin was.

G-Mags stirred her pot and put the cover back on. "I remember that movie. I had a little bit of a crush on the actor who starred in it."

"That's gross," Kevin said.

"Now, what's gross about that?" G-Mags asked. "You wouldn't be here if I hadn't had a crush on your grandfather and married him." She stopped, bowed her head, and added, "May he rest in peace."

Kevin's grandfather had died a long time ago. Still, G-Mags always got this misty look in her eyes every time she talked about him. When that happened, Kevin would change the subject or make her laugh. This time he removed the cover from the pot and said, "Mmmm, smells good."

"I used my secret ingredient," G-Mags said. She pointed to a large clay pot with several leafy green stalks growing out of it.

I leaned toward the plant and inhaled. It had a sweet smell with a touch of freshly mown grass thrown in. "What is it?" I asked.

"It's rosemary. Years ago, I got this ragout recipe from my sister, Eleanor." G-Mags bowed her head and whispered, "May she rest in peace."

G-Mags said this a lot, which led me to believe she knew a lot of dead people. And she must have been worried there was something keeping them from having a peaceful afterlife.

I caught another whiff of rosemary and held my breath. I wanted to capture the smell—and everything else I loved about that place.

"Oh dear." G-Mags put her hand to her forehead and collapsed into a kitchen chair.

Kevin ran to her.

She waved him off. "It's just a little dizzy spell. I should have eaten something earlier."

Kevin and I let her rest while we set the table. After a few minutes she felt better and dished out the ragout.

"Hey," Kevin said as we brought the dishes to the table, "bet you can't spell ragout."

Kevin was a champion speller and loved that he could always beat me at a challenge. I thought for a minute. "R-a-g-o-o?"

"Ha! I knew you'd say that. It's r-a-g-o-u-t."

At that moment, Mr. Damico came in from the backyard and chimed in, "It's from a French word, meaning 'to revive the taste.'"

Mrs. Damico rolled her eyes. "You know the reason they call it 'trivia' is because it's trivial?" Even though she was smiling, she had the look of someone who had heard the same thing way too many times.

Kevin put the last of the napkins on the table, and we all began to eat. I savored each mouthful, knowing that I might never taste it again. Mom and Dad had said we probably wouldn't spend next summer at the shore. And G-Mags was thinking about selling her cottage and moving into an assisted living facility. "I think I can taste the rosemary," I said.

G-Mags smiled and put her hand on my shoulder. "It's a symbol of remembrance."

Mr. Damico held his fork in the air. "Did you know early Greek students took the meaning literally and wore wreaths of rosemary on their heads in order to stimulate their memories during exams?"

Kevin's eyes brightened. "Did it work?"

Mr. Damico laughed and said he didn't think it was as effective as studying.

I'm sure he was right. But just in case, G-Mags gave Kevin and me a few stalks of rosemary to take home with us.

Now whenever I smell rosemary, I think of summer.

CHAPTER 8

"Have you finished packing yet?" Mom called from the living room.

"Not yet." I figured I'd organize my backpack first and shook the contents onto the rug. There was the rosemary, a tube of sunscreen, some hand sanitizer from Mom, a *Star Wars* video I kept forgetting to give back to Kevin, a bunch of sand, my beach towel, wallet, phone, sketchpad, colored pencils, and . . . a flat rectangular box I didn't recognize.

I picked it up and examined it. The yellow cardboard

was faded and scratched. On one side, printed in black, were the words MAGIC PAINTS.

The seal on the box had already been broken. I pried open the flap and pulled out a thin canvas about the size of a piece of notebook paper. A tube of black paint fell out. It was dented in the middle and looked as if it had already been used. After running my hand around the inside of the box, I found a palette, brushes, linseed oil, and more paint. I spread it all out on my bed. Bits of silver peeked through lines and cracks where the tubes had been squeezed.

Some small print on the back of the carton read:

Contents include: two canvases, nine tubes of paint, two brushes, one palette, and a bottle of linseed oil for thinning paint.

I suspected the original owner had used the missing canvas. Bringing the box even closer, I read the tiny letters at the bottom: *Paint your heart's desire.*

Someone had to have put the box in my backpack by mistake. I felt bad for the person who lost the paints. But I was leaving the next day—there was no time to find the owner.

I wondered what he or she had painted on the missing canvas. I held up the remaining one and ran my hand across its rough surface.

My fingertips tingled. I remembered the beach scene from earlier that day.

After placing the canvas on my desk, I picked up the palette and squirted a blob of blue paint on it. Then a drop of white. A fire ignited inside me as I inhaled the sharp smell of oil and mixed the colors with a brush to create the perfect tint. I attacked the canvas with thick clumps of paint and then swirled it all around.

When I finished with the sky, I added some green to the mix. With several quick brushstrokes, the ocean appeared. Next, I mixed yellow, brown, and white for the shoreline and the sand sculptures. Finally, I added several drops of black to the palette for the stick-figure bodies lying in the sun.

When the painting was finished, I scrawled my name on the lower right side of the canvas and hid it along with the paint box on the floor of my closet.

Mom's germ phobia was out of control, and I figured if she saw the old box and paints, she would have made me throw it all in the trash.

A few minutes later, just for fun, I opened the closet and looked at the painting again, remembering the words on the box.

Squeezing my eyes shut, I took a deep breath and wished for a mulligan of my last day of summer.

CHAPTER 9

After realizing I'd packed all my pajamas, I crawled into bed, wearing my shorts and T-shirt. I rolled over to one side and stared at the wall. The light from the streetlamp cast shadows of shimmying leaves. Reaching out to trace them with my finger, I thought about how those leaves would be gone in a few months.

That was the last thing I remembered before being woken up by the doorbell.

Ringing and ringing and ringing.

I jumped out of bed. The sound of my parents

scurrying to the front door filled the silences between chimes. By the time I reached the living room, my mother, wearing her blue bathrobe with the belt trailing behind, was deep in conversation with Kevin's parents on the porch. My father stood behind my mother, listening and nodding, while my heart kicked against my rib cage. Where was Kevin?

I ran to my mother's side and yanked the door open wider.

Relief swept over me as Kevin stepped forward from behind his dad. Beyond the porch, a crescent moon and stars were the only signs of light. Why were the Damicos on our doorstep at this hour? Amid my confusion, the words "mother" and "stroke" penetrated the fuzziness in my brain. And then I understood.

It was G-Mags.

Words that sounded like a foreign language spouted from my mother's mouth. "How bad is it? Do you need us to drive you to the hospital?" And "Of course Kevin can stay here." Mom moved to the side so Kevin could fit through the doorway with his backpack and pillow. "We'll take good care of him," she said. "Don't worry."

For the first time all summer, I had no idea what to

say to Kevin. He looked so different, standing in the living room in his T-shirt and shorts, hugging his pillow. Even the Tweety Bird Band-Aid G-Mags had put on his scraped knee looked sad.

Finally, Mom broke the silence and asked me to get sheets and a blanket for the couch.

I dashed to the closet, nearly knocking over the three packed suitcases in the hall. When I got back to the living room, Kevin was sitting at the kitchen table. Mom handed him a glass of water. I could tell by the slope of her shoulders that even *she* didn't know how to make Kevin feel better.

I took my time spreading the sheets and blanket, smoothing out each wrinkle. Finally, when every crease was pressed and every corner tucked, I joined Kevin and Mom at the table.

Pink splotches dotted Kevin's face, matching the color in his cried-out eyes. He grabbed a napkin from the holder and blew his nose. "The paramedics said they couldn't tell if she'd be okay."

Mom took Kevin's empty glass to the sink. "I'm sure the doctors will do everything they can for her."

Kevin squeezed his eyes shut for a few seconds and nodded.

"We should all go to bed and get some sleep," Mom said. She turned to Kevin. "Your parents said they'd call in the morning—as soon as they know something." She smiled with her mouth but not her eyes.

I followed Kevin to the couch. "If the AC gets too cold in here, just knock on my door. I'll give you another blanket—I don't usually need mine."

He nodded.

"I'm sorry," I whispered. "I hope she'll be okay."

Kevin pulled the covers up to his chin and closed his eyes, as if he wanted to shut out the world.

I wished there were something I could do.

But I couldn't think of anything.

CHAPTER 10

Slamming the alarm button down, I narrowed my eyes at the bright red numbers: 7:00. Hadn't I flipped the switch to off after I went back to bed last night? Still in a morning fog, I stared at the numbers as they changed to 7:01.

Tugging at the sheet coiled around my leg, I tried to go back to sleep. But I couldn't stop thinking about Kevin.

I crawled out of bed and crept toward the living room. Beyond the hallway, the sun spilled through the blinds, creating a pattern of light and dark lines on the carpet.

As I turned the corner, the couch came into view.

It was empty.

Kevin was gone. And so were the sheets and blanket. I looked around for his pillow and backpack. They were gone too.

Had his parents come to get him already?

I checked the front door. Locked. The only way Kevin could have left was if someone had let him out and locked the door behind him. Had the Damicos come for Kevin in the middle of the night?

Why would they come to get him before morning? Why not wait? Was G-Mags back home? Or was she . . . ?

Taking a deep breath, I headed toward my parents' bedroom for answers. I was halfway down the hall when I remembered something. Where was all the luggage that had been sitting next to the hallway entrance?

Had Dad put the suitcases in the car in the middle of the night? Why would he pack up the car in the dark?

I ran to my room to see if my own suitcase was still by my door. It wasn't. I opened my dresser drawers. Everything was still folded neatly inside.

I pressed my fingers against my temples. The

luggage wasn't in the hall. My clothes weren't packed. And Kevin was gone.

I tiptoed to my parents' room and tapped Mom's shoulder. "Where's Kevin?" I whispered. "And where's all the luggage?"

Mom opened one eye into a tiny slit as I repeated the question. She hoisted herself up and leaned against the headboard. "Isn't he at his grandmother's?"

"I don't know. Did his parents come for him?"

"Come for him? Wasn't he at his grandmother's when you left after dinner?"

Why was Mom asking these questions? "Of course he was there when I left. But he was on our couch last time we saw him."

"Our couch? Sweetie, you must have dreamt he came over."

Was Mom so tired she forgot what happened? She *had* been more forgetful than usual. "Okay, never mind about Kevin," I said. "Where are all our packed suitcases?"

Mom stared at me for a second and smiled.

My eyes locked on hers. "This is serious."

"I think I know what's going on," she said. "You had a wish fulfillment dream."

"What's that?"

"It's when you dream something that you wish would happen."

No way would I have wished G-Mags had a stroke.

Mom took my hand and continued, "You and Kevin have become such good friends, I bet you wish he could come home with us tomorrow."

"Tomorrow? Aren't we leaving today?"

"For someone who never wanted to leave the shore, you're certainly pushing things."

"What do you mean?"

"We don't leave until tomorrow. We have all day today."

"We do?"

Mom shook her head. "That must have been some dream you had. You better change out of those pajamas if you're going to meet Kevin."

Just as she said that, I looked down and gasped. I'd gone to sleep in my shorts and T-shirt. Where had those pajamas come from?

I darted to the kitchen to check the calendar. The day before I'd torn off the page that read *26* and thrown it away. I stopped short when I saw the number *26* staring at me.

Maybe I was remembering wrong. Maybe the sheet I'd thrown away read 25. I took a step closer to see the Fun Animal Fact at the bottom of the page. My heart drummed faster and faster as I read the words: *A mayfly has an average life expectancy of twenty-four hours.*

It was the same fun fact as the day before.

CHAPTER 11

The second I hit the boardwalk, I spotted Kevin walking toward me with a smile on his face. He was wearing the same clothes as the day before: a red, white, and blue Captain America T-shirt and white shorts.

I looked him up and down for clues and then moved closer to smell his clothes for a sign that he'd already worn them. I got a whiff of lilac detergent as my face banged into his shoulder.

"What are you doing?" He grabbed hold of his shirt

and brought it to his nose. "Did I pull this out of the wrong laundry basket?"

I shook my head. "You're fine. I just had a weird feeling."

"That my shirt would smell?"

"No. Like we did this all before."

"You mean reincarnation?"

"No. Like yesterday morning we did the exact same thing."

"We probably did. We've been doing the same thing every morning for almost eight weeks. I thought maybe you had a vision of us as a king and queen in a past life or something. That would be awesome."

"Yeah, awesome," I said as I caught sight of Kevin's knee. There was no Tweety Bird Band-Aid. And no scab. He couldn't have healed that quickly.

Was Mom right? Had I dreamt a whole day?

"So, what do you want for breakfast?" Kevin said. "I'm in the mood for one of Annie's egg and sausage bagels."

My mouth dropped open. "That's *exactly* what you said in the dream I had last night."

"Whoooo, spooky."

"It's not funny."

"It is, really, considering I've had an egg and sausage bagel for breakfast a bunch of times this summer."

"I guess you're right."

Heading through the door of Annie's Ark, we were greeted with the familiar smell of bacon, along with the sound of the local oldies station playing softly amid the chatter of early-morning diners.

Soon, Annie strolled over to our booth. Her dark hair was pulled back into a tight bun, and her eyeliner was painted way past the end of her lid on one side, exactly like in my dream. "What can I get for you two this morning?" she asked.

When we told her it was our last whole day down the shore, she got a little misty-eyed and sat next to me. "I'm really going to miss you two," she said. "You remind me of when my Joey was your age." She gestured toward the grill, where Joey was cooking up orders. "You kids just grow up too fast—soon Joey will be taking over the Ark. It seems like yesterday . . ."

As her voice trailed off, I looked over at Joey, who wore a hairnet over his short ponytail. He flipped a pancake high into the air. Cringing, I waited for what would happen next.

Splat!

The pancake landed on the floor, just like I'd anticipated. Annie smiled. "Maybe it'll be a little while longer before Joey's ready to take over."

I wasn't sure if it was the smell of burnt toast or the fact that Annie had said the exact same thing in my dream that made me break out into a cold sweat. But the minute she finished taking our order, I excused myself to go to the bathroom and put water on my face.

By the time I got back, the food was already on the table. "You're really just having orange juice?" Kevin said.

"My stomach's a little queasy."

"Are you okay? We can leave if—"

"No. It's nothing serious."

"That's good," Kevin said. "It'd be awful if we had to skip our last day at the shore together."

I forced a smile and mumbled, "It sure would."

CHAPTER 12

Once we left Annie's, we stopped to look at Serena's sketches. Serena was a college student who paid for some of her tuition by drawing portraits of people on the boardwalk. She had long, strawberry blond hair and freckles that spread across her nose and cheeks like flecks of sand. Every day she wore a different hat. She said it was because the sun gave her even more freckles. But I liked to think it was an artistic statement. That day's hat was familiar. It was straw with a huge brim that held a bunch of grapes on one side and a banana on the other.

The little girl sitting across from Serena seemed familiar too. She was about six years old and wore a headband with a red and white polka-dot bow. Her mother pressed the girl's shoulder down to keep her from getting up from the wooden stool. Apparently, this girl had no interest in preserving *that* particular moment in a painting.

While Serena struggled with the portrait, I headed toward her table of artwork for sale. She loved to start drawing before dawn, and her new works were always at the top of the pile. When I spotted the pastel sketch of a dark sky and stars above the ocean waves, I stumbled backward in surprise. I'd already seen that one.

"You okay?" Serena asked between brushstrokes.

"I'm fine. But when did you draw this?"

"Before sunrise," Serena said. "The sky was so clear, and the stars were gorgeous."

Kevin stared at me. "Are you sure you're okay? You just got really pale."

"I'm sure," I answered, even though I was more confused than ever. "It's just the heat."

After browsing in Mr. Sidhu's used book and video store, Kevin and I headed toward the water. Once we passed the familiar crying toddler, the boys tossing the football, and the sunbathers lying on the beach, we settled into our spot by the pier. A slight fishy smell breezed by as I spread my towel out on the sand and anchored one corner with my backpack.

"Hey, guys," a voice from behind us called. I turned to find Mateo heading toward us. His parents sat under a big beach umbrella, not too far away. "Want to build a sand castle?"

Kevin smiled at him. "Sure. In a little while."

Mateo, who was nine years old, had been our shadow all summer. "Hey, listen to this one," he said. "Why should you take your clock to the bank?"

I groaned before answering. "You just told us that one yesterday: to save time."

Mateo scrunched his face into a pout. "I never told you that one. I just got it this morning—from a Popsicle stick I found on the boardwalk."

"First of all, *ew,* that you picked up a strange Popsicle stick. And second, bringing your clock to the bank would actually *take up* valuable time for no reason, *not* save time."

Mateo looked at Kevin for support.

"Dude, she's got a point. But I don't remember you telling it yesterday." He turned to me. "You must have heard it somewhere else."

I was sure I hadn't, but I didn't want to talk about it anymore. I pulled my T-shirt off and shimmied out of my shorts, determined to have fun. "Race you to the water!" I shouted.

Kevin chased me, yelling, "Cheater!" He dashed by me and dove into a huge wave.

I swam out and flipped onto my back. My mind wandered as the ocean rocked me from side to side. I thought about how great it was that I still had this whole day with Kevin. But as much as I tried to forget, the memory of him and his parents standing on our doorstep kept pushing its way into my thoughts.

When I lifted my head, Kevin was several yards away, waving in my direction. The surf had taken me farther out than we usually went. I waved and raced back to shore. By the time I got there, Kevin and Mateo were molding a pile of wet sand. "Hey, I'm the artist around here," I said. "You couldn't wait before you started making the stegosaurus?"

Kevin squinted up at me. "How did you know we were making a stegosaurus?"

The swell of sand by my feet was just a blob. I collapsed onto my knees and began scooping large handfuls of sand onto the mound. "Lucky guess," I lied.

"C'mon," Mateo said. "Let's make it *huge*."

We worked for nearly a half hour, molding the stegosaurus's head, body, and tail. When we were done with that, I grabbed a plastic bucket and headed toward the ocean. As I filled the container, voices behind me grew louder. I turned to find a couple of girls I'd seen before on the beach. One of them pointed to Kevin and Mateo and giggled. "I can't believe we used to do that." She threw her long, dark hair back over her shoulder. I looked down at my bucket. She was just like those girls at school who couldn't think of anything else but clothes and makeup. I gritted my teeth, remembering I'd felt that same way the day before—or was it in the dream?

I hauled the pail back to the stegosaurus, and Kevin smiled up at me. I instantly forgot about those girls and dumped the water onto the beach. "Watch," I said, squeezing a fistful of sand into my palm. My nails dug

into my skin for a second before I released my fingers to reveal a tiny disk. "See. A spike." I placed it on the spine of the dinosaur.

Mateo's eyes widened. "Cool! I want to make some."

I handed him a glob of sand. "Go ahead. We need a whole bunch of them." As we worked together, I tried to get the vision of the two girls out of my head. What was so childish about what I was doing? Why couldn't I still have fun sculpting a dinosaur on the beach?

Once Kevin set the last spike in place, he announced, "Done!"

"It's just like the one in my painting," I said without thinking.

Kevin looked up. "What painting?"

"Oh," I mumbled. "Last night I painted a picture of a sand stegosaurus." But as soon as the words came out of my mouth, I wondered: Had I painted the stegosaurus or just dreamt it?

Before I could think more about it, Kevin began filming the dinosaur and instructed Mateo and me to act scared and run down the beach. He followed us as we raced along the shore, screaming.

A few minutes later, he shouted, "That's a wrap!

Rise of the Zombie Stegosauruses. Watch for it at your local theater."

Mateo gave Kevin a big smile and a thumbs-up.

After we left the beach, the next few hours felt awfully familiar—the cow suit, the cannolis, Kevin's suggestion to go to Atlantic City.

As I headed back to our house to get ready, I recapped what I'd thought had been the previous day. I'd been positive the Damicos had knocked on our door with that terrible news. And even though I hadn't checked my closet before I left, I was pretty sure I'd found the paint set and used it. But there was no real evidence that any of those things had happened.

My head spun with theories. No matter what was happening to me, there had to be some good reason for it.

And then it hit me: I was supposed to save G-Mags!

CHAPTER 13

I burst through the door of our cottage and rushed past Dad to get ready for Atlantic City. I was on a mission. A mission to save G-Mags.

It was all so clear. As soon as I got a chance, I would somehow convince her that she should go to the doctor. Then everything would be fine.

The second I got to my room, I checked the closet to see if the painting was there. It wasn't. I guessed that was one portion of the dream that hadn't come true.

I showered in record time and looked up some things about strokes on Mom's laptop in the kitchen.

When I was through, I still had time before the Damicos were coming. I pulled up a chair next to Dad. "Have you ever had a dream that came true in real life?"

He peered up at me through his glasses. "I can't say that I have. But I do think dreams can change the future."

"You do?"

He gestured to the papers on his desk. "Take Albert Einstein, for example. Legend has it that his dream about cows changed the future of science."

"Cows?" A picture of Kevin in his costume came to mind, and I had to laugh.

Dad nodded. "Einstein supposedly dreamt about cows lined up against an electric fence. When the farmer turned the electricity on, Einstein saw all the cows jump back at the same time. He explained what he saw to the farmer, who had been across the field. But the farmer argued with Einstein, saying the cows jumped away one at a time."

"So how did that affect the future of science?"

"Einstein wasn't content to do nothing about the dream. He thought about it—a lot. He finally came to the conclusion that events look different, depending on where the viewer is standing."

"But why does that happen?"

"It has to do with the amount of time it takes for light to reach the eye. Many believe the dream influenced Einstein's theory of relativity." Dad leaned back in his chair. "So you see, his dream might have changed the future of how scientists looked at space and time."

I wasn't sure I could be like Einstein and come up with a new theory about the universe, but I hoped my dream could help me change the future for G-Mags.

Once I was in the car with the Damicos, I tried to figure out a way to bring up the symptoms of a stroke without sounding weird. After looking it up on the Internet, I was pretty sure G-Mags's dizzy spell was a sign that something was wrong. I cleared my throat. "Um . . ."

"Yes, Haleigh," Mrs. Damico said, turning toward the backseat.

"I, uh, was just wondering how G-Mags is doing."

"She's getting a little gardening in while we're gone."

"But how is she feeling?"

"Very well, thank you. It's nice of you to ask." She

turned forward and began directing Mr. Damico toward the correct road to take.

How could I talk them into taking G-Mags to the doctor when nothing was wrong yet? I decided to bring it up again when we got back. After all, G-Mags had been fine until just before dinner.

Once we arrived at the hotel, Mrs. Damico gave us her instructions, and Kevin pulled me toward the taco place.

As we took our seats, I looked for the guy I'd dreamt about, the one who had been sitting behind me. The chair was empty. Looking down at the menu, I felt a little better. If there was no man there and no painting in my room, then not everything in the dream was coming true. Maybe G-Mags would be fine after all.

But then . . . I spotted the man with his briefcase. He passed us and sat behind me.

After a minute or two Kevin blew the paper on his straw across the table. I caught it and rolled it up into a tiny ball.

Kevin's eyes opened wide. "Wow! Good reflexes."

I smiled, secretly hoping that saving G-Mags would be as easy as catching that paper.

After we finished lunch, Kevin and I moved on to the shops and then to mini golf. With each hole, I tried to convince myself that even though almost everything was the same as in my dream, it didn't mean G-Mags would have a stroke at the end of the day.

When it took me only four tries instead of six to hit the ball between Humpty Dumpty's legs, I jumped up and down.

"There's still no way you can win," Kevin said.

I shrugged and gave him a smile. My excitement had nothing to do with changing my score, but everything to do with changing the future.

As soon as we were through, Kevin took the clubs up to the front counter. This time I grabbed my backpack and hurried behind him. The second he stepped onto the boardwalk, I spotted the rickshaw bicyclist headed straight at us. My hand flew out, almost as if it weren't mine, and yanked Kevin out of the way just in time.

"Whoa, thanks!" he said.

I stared at the back of the rickshaw as it kept going. "I'd almost forgotten about him."

"What do you mean?"

"Uh, nothing. I just saw him before and he was driving recklessly." I clutched my backpack and strolled into the hotel. Everything that had happened so far seemed to mean one thing: if I could improve my golf score and save Kevin from a scraped knee, there was a good chance I could prevent G-Mags from having a stroke.

CHAPTER 14

While Kevin watched the movie, my eyes were fixed on G-Mags. She looked out the window, stirring her stew as if nothing was wrong.

"Why don't you sit?" I asked her. "I'll take over the ragout."

She waved me toward the table. "I don't need to sit. I'm perfectly capable of cooking dinner, but you can keep me company if you'd like."

I sat on a kitchen chair, close to her. It felt weird to think something terrible might happen, and I was just waiting. Like I was the only one who knew there was a hurricane coming, and I should have been yelling out, "Close all the windows! Hide in the closet!" Instead, I was watching everybody go through their normal routines. It didn't seem right.

I clutched the cell phone in my pocket.

Then, just like in my dream, G-Mags went to get the silverware and had her dizzy spell.

I jumped up from the chair. "Please!" I shouted. "Let me call 911."

Everyone turned to me with the same puzzled look. The urgency in my voice had scared them. But not for the right reason.

Kevin looked away from the TV and asked if I was okay.

"It's G-Mags," I said. "She needs a doctor."

"I'm fine, dear, really," she said. "It's just a little dizzy spell."

I bit my upper lip and nodded, feeling foolish.

Kevin turned to me. "You've been acting weird all day. Are you okay?"

I forced a smile. I wanted to tell him what was bothering me, but it would have sounded crazy. And with Mr. Damico being a psychologist and all, I certainly didn't want to seem crazy.

Minutes later, G-Mags was fine.

Still, before I met Dad outside to walk me home, I leaned toward her and whispered, "Promise me you'll call the doctor if you get another one of your spells."

"I will," she said. Then she handed me a container with a leftover cannoli inside and added, "Make sure you stop by before you leave tomorrow morning. I have something else for you."

I wasn't sure what would happen later or if I'd done enough to warn G-Mags. But I could feel the ragout bubbling up in my stomach as I walked home with Dad.

CHAPTER 15

Fifteen minutes later, I walked into my room and screamed.

Mom ran to see what happened.

I pointed to the painting resting on the yellow box on my desk. “Where did this come from?”

“I found it in your closet this morning,” Mom said. “I put it on the porch for a while—in the sun. I thought you’d packed up your oil paints before we left for the shore.”

“Uh, no,” I lied, studying the blue swirls, the sand stegosaurus, the stick figures. It was definitely my work. But I hadn't painted anything that day. Finding the yellow box in my backpack was the one part of the dream that hadn't come true.

So how did this painting get here?

Mom examined the canvas and smiled. "It's beautiful. You've captured everything perfectly."

"You always say that."

"And you can believe it. I'm an expert, you know." Mom's an art history professor and had been working on a book about van Gogh all summer.

"Yeah," I said. "I know."

"You better leave that out." Mom gestured toward the canvas. "Oils can take weeks to dry."

I nodded, still staring at the picture. If I'd actually used the paints, did that mean I hadn't been dreaming after all, that when I'd painted my heart's desire for a mulligan . . . I'd gotten my wish?

There was no other explanation.

I thought for a few minutes. Hearts could have more than one desire. Couldn't they?

I gazed at the painting, squeezed my eyes shut, and wished that G-Mags wouldn't have a stroke.

I'd warned her earlier. I'd suggested that the

Damicos call 911. And now I'd wished on the painting.

Would that be enough to change the future?

Unable to sleep, I watched the clock's red numbers change: 10:15, 10:16, 10:17. What time had the doorbell rung before? I couldn't remember. Rolling over to face my desk, I caught sight of the painting one more time before drifting off to sleep.

Within what seemed like minutes, I leaped out of bed.

The doorbell echoed as I headed to the living room, praying I'd encounter something different from before. A doorbell in the middle of the night didn't always mean trouble. Did it? Maybe it was good news. Like my parents won the lottery or something. Why hadn't I wished for that?

Darkness filled the living room as the words I dreaded echoed in my ears.

Again, Kevin's eyes were tinged with sadness.

I stood frozen, unable to think of any words to help him. What followed was exactly as I'd remembered: the sheets, the blanket, the water. Then back to my room.

As I lay in bed and stared at the ceiling, my eyes stung.

How could my wish have given me a whole extra day with Kevin but not allowed me to change something as important as G-Mags's stroke?

At the sound of the alarm, I jumped out of bed and looked at the clock's red numerals: 7:00. I rubbed my eyes and got a heavy feeling in my stomach. Kevin would be on the couch this time, and G-Mags would be in the hospital. I was sure you could have only one mulligan in life. If you ever got one at all.

I tiptoed through the hallway, turned the corner into the living room, and nearly fell over the couch.

Kevin was gone!

I dashed to the kitchen to look at the calendar. Swallowing hard, I stared at the number *26* and the words: *A mayfly has an average life expectancy of twenty-four hours.*

Although I was more confused than ever, I decided not to wake Mom this time. What would I say?

I headed back to my room and examined the painting. It was still shiny and wet. Bringing it closer, I inhaled the smell of the paint and linseed oil.

My pulse raced. Could I be getting another do-over?

CHAPTER 16

I studied G-Mags from across the table and tried to think of how to warn her.

As I laid the rubber spatula on the spoon rest, an idea came to me. "Next week before school starts, I have to get a physical," I announced.

"I already went," Kevin said. "I grew two inches since last year."

I looked at G-Mags. "When was the last time you went to the doctor?"

"At my age I'm at the doctor's office more times a year than I can count."

"Maybe," I said, "it would be a good idea to go today."

Kevin gave me a weird look.

"Don't I look well?" G-Mags said, patting her curls. "Maybe I'm having a bad hair day."

"Oh, no. It's just that . . . my mom has an appointment at the doctor when we get home, so I've just been thinking about good health."

"She's in great health," Kevin chimed in. He turned to G-Mags. "Aren't you?"

"Don't you worry about me." She placed the last cannoli shell on the counter to cool.

I took a deep breath and blinked until my eyes stopped stinging.

As I pushed through our cottage door, my frustration grew. Dad's notebooks and papers were scattered all over the desk. I hated to disturb him, but I had to.

I tapped his shoulder, and for a second he was startled.

"Sorry," I said. "I was just wondering . . . have you ever had a day where you felt like you'd lived through that whole twenty-four hours already?"

Dad swiveled his desk chair toward me. "You mean like déjà vu?"

"It's more than that. It's like the whole day is almost *exactly* the same as yesterday."

Dad stroked his beard. "You mean like a time loop?"

"What's a time loop?"

"I guess you could explain it like a clock that goes backward and keeps resetting itself."

"Is that a real thing?"

"I read a short story once about a man who kept experiencing the same hour over and over again. It was called '12:01 P.M.' No matter what the man did, after an hour the clock would spring back to 12:01 p.m. and he would live that hour over again."

Was that what was happening to me? "How long did that go on?"

Dad shook his head. "I read the story about fifteen years ago. I don't remember the ending."

My skin prickled. "Could people go back in time in real life?"

Dad leaned back in his chair and laughed. "No. But according to Einstein's theory of time dilation, time would run slower for someone traveling close to the speed of light. So, if you were in a spaceship traveling that fast for four years, when you came back to Earth, more than sixty years might have passed for everyone who stayed on the ground."

"Wow. That would be weird. I'd be sixteen, but you'd be more than a hundred." A twinge of dizziness came over me. I wasn't sure if it was Einstein's theory or the thought of Dad being that old.

Later, when I played Scrabble with Kevin and the Damicos, I got another idea about how to help G-Mags. When no one was looking, I lifted the receiver off the landline in the kitchen and punched in 911. I knew the number could be traced, and an ambulance would be there in a little while, even if I didn't say anything into the phone.

I took tiny bites of my cannoli as I kept my eyes fixed on the front door, waiting for the paramedics to arrive. I was almost done when there was a knock. Mr. Damico answered it.

"We received a call from this house," a man in a uniform said. "Everything okay?"

Mr. Damico looked around the room. "Looks like it."

"Are you sure?" the man asked.

I held my breath as his eyes lingered on mine. Could he tell I was the one who called?

"It must be some mistake," Mr. Damico said.

I whispered to G-Mags, "Maybe you should go with them, to see about your dizziness."

"Don't be silly," she said. "I'm fine."

"You're positive everyone is okay?" the paramedic said.

G-Mags went to the door. "My son is right. There must be some mistake."

As I watched the guy head toward his truck, I got a sick feeling inside. Wasn't there anything I could do to help G-Mags?

CHAPTER 17

The next day, the same thing happened. And the next. And the next. At first I thought the day kept repeating so I could eventually talk G-Mags into going to the hospital. But after a couple of weeks of living the same day over and over, it was pretty clear she was never going with the paramedics. Finally, I stopped dialing 911.

More time passed, and I started thinking it was a good thing the day kept repeating. Each morning, G-Mags was fine. Who knew what would happen if time moved forward?

And would it be so bad to live in a never-ending summer? To not have to deal with seventh grade? There were definitely advantages: no teachers telling me to put away my sketchbook, no homework, no mean girls, no pimples.

And then there was Kevin. We'd stay friends forever—nothing would change us. Not time, not distance, not different schools.

One afternoon as Dad was explaining to me how black holes form when a star explodes at the end of its life cycle, I couldn't help but smile. The life cycle didn't appear to be ending for G-Mags—or anyone else, for that matter.

When the Damicos' car horn sounded from the driveway, Mom threw me the apple like she did every day. I caught it, threw it back, and bounded out the door with an energy I hadn't felt in a while.

The neon taco sign glowed in front of me as I thought about having Mexican food again. Riffling through my wallet, I was still amazed that my money kept reappearing.

"What are you smiling about?" Kevin asked.

"Nothing." I grabbed his arm. "C'mon, I'll buy you a quesadilla."

As we talked, I realized I could change some things about the day, like our conversations and some of our activities. But other things were always exactly the same: the waitress with her flamingo pink lipstick, the eavesdropping man with the briefcase, Marty the magician and his trick with the scarf.

Throughout the day, the sameness of things was comforting. Especially when I was back in G-Mags's kitchen, smelling the rosemary all over again.

"Hey," Kevin said, "bet you can't spell ragout."

Without thinking, I spelled out, "R-a-g-o-u-t."

Kevin looked disappointed. "How did you know that? I would have bet money you'd spell it wrong."

"I must have seen it somewhere." I wasn't really lying. Was I?

Once the ragout was dished out, I wondered if I would ever get tired of eating the same thing for dinner every night. I pierced a piece of meat with my fork and swirled it around in the juices. Ragout every night was a small price to pay for a never-ending summer.

• • •

Back in my room that night, I picked up the canvas on my desk and touched the sky. A bit of blue paint came off on my fingertip. I rubbed it away and looked over at my suitcase on the bed. For a minute I considered not packing. Then I realized Mom might get suspicious.

She poked her head in on the way to bed. "See you in the morning," she said, smiling.

"Um, yeah," I said. "See you in the morning." But, of course, I saw her before that.

Oddly, even though Kevin was as miserable as he'd been the previous times, my own sadness wasn't as strong. Knowing this night was like chalk on a blackboard and would all be erased the next day was almost exhilarating, like I'd won some kind of time loop lottery.

Just thinking about it made me too restless to sleep. Once everyone was quiet, I raced to the refrigerator and took out the cannoli G-Mags had given me earlier. Knowing that another one would take its place the next night, I took a huge bite.

Sweet!

CHAPTER 18

Kevin picked up the same box of saltwater taffy that he'd shown me every day. I pretended I hadn't seen it before. I'd gotten to be an expert at acting as if everything were brand-new. Seriously, I could have won an Academy Award.

I'd considered telling Kevin what was going on, but I suspected he wouldn't understand. He'd think I was either joking or losing my mind. Kevin believed in tricks. Illusions. Like Marty's sleight of hand. But he didn't believe in magic.

He held the candy box in front of me. "Want some? My treat."

I was about to say I didn't want to break a bracket on my braces. But instead, I answered, "Sure!" Why hadn't I thought of it before? Even if I broke a bracket, it would be fixed the next morning.

Once Kevin paid for the box, I surveyed the multi-colored taffy. Reaching first for the green one, I changed my mind and went for the red. The spicy cinnamon was sweet and hot at the same time. Delicious. Several chews later, a wire snapped. Metal scraped the inside of my mouth, but I kept on chewing without saying a word. Kevin might have wondered why I took a chance—I'd been talking about that prize from the orthodontist all summer long. I swept my tongue along the inside of my cheek. The skin was ragged. Still, I grabbed another piece of taffy and popped it in my mouth. I could handle the sting till morning.

After the usual nighttime ringing of the doorbell, I turned down the covers on the couch for Kevin. The look on his face made me want to tell him everything.

That G-Mags would be fine in the morning. That, somehow, time had stopped—just like in that sci-fi movie we'd been watching every day. That we would never have to worry about sickness. Or dying.

He looked so miserable as he pulled the blanket up to his chin. Instead of rushing off to my room, I sat on the floor and whispered, "It'll be okay."

"The paramedics said it looked serious," Kevin said, his voice cracking.

I drew my knees to my chest and hugged them. "But G-Mags is tough. Remember those stories she told us about how poor she was? How her family hardly had any food—and there was no medicine when she got sick? She's a survivor." I knew it wasn't the same as surviving a stroke, but I wanted so much to make Kevin feel better.

His eyes brightened and he gave a tiny smile. "She *is* tough, isn't she?"

"Sure she is."

Seconds passed, and the brightness faded. "People can die from strokes," he said. "Or become paralyzed for the rest of their lives."

"But it doesn't always happen. I've heard of people

having strokes and being okay afterward. I'm sure G-Mags will be fine in the morning."

Kevin rolled sideways, away from me. "You can't be sure."

I clasped my knees tighter. "But I am sure."

"How?"

"I don't know. I just feel it."

After a few minutes of silence, I tiptoed to my bedroom. There was no use trying to explain things. I didn't even understand what was going on myself.

Once I was in my bed, I stared out the window at the same wispy moon I'd seen behind Kevin's parents each night. I knew from science class that it was a waxing crescent moon, which meant it was moving toward being full.

I studied it a little longer, imagining it as the final curve in a pair of parentheses, the close of a single thought, suspended in the infinite sky.

CHAPTER 19

When the clock rang at seven, the first thing I did was to stretch my tongue toward my back teeth. Yes! No broken bracket. The inside of my cheek was as smooth as a baby's.

Later, when Kevin and I visited Mr. Sidhu's shop, I realized it had to have been several weeks since the time loop started. I was pretty familiar with the inventory on those floor-to-ceiling shelves, and I'd read quite a few of the books.

I passed a table filled with mystery novels, squeezed together like a deck of cards. A similar table marked

ROMANCE sat across from Mr. Sidhu, who was behind the counter, reading a worn-out paperback with an old-fashioned spaceship on the front.

While Kevin talked to Mr. Sidhu, I browsed through the kids' mystery novels. It was the third day in a row I was buying the same book about a stolen painting. I planned on finishing it that night. I had my eye on another mystery for the next day. That one had a shadow, a shoe, and a key on the cover.

When I brought my book to the counter, Kevin was deep in conversation with Mr. Sidhu. As he listened, Mr. Sidhu's bushy, black eyebrows moved up and down. He was saying what he said every day—even before the time loop started—that the DVD set Kevin wanted was $59.99.

Kevin stuck his hand in his pocket and frowned. "I don't have that much money."

Mr. Sidhu looked sympathetic. "Do you have a birthday coming up? Maybe you can make a list. Put these on it."

Kevin shook his head. "It's not until October."

"I am sorry," Mr. Sidhu said. "But I cannot change the price. This is a collector's item. But I will tell you what I can do. If anyone comes here and shows an interest in the DVDs, I will give you a call first. You can let me know if you have saved up enough money to buy them." He handed Kevin a card to write on.

"But I live more than an hour away."

"Do not worry," Mr. Sidhu said. "I will hold them for you."

"Wow, thanks. I'll start saving my allowance as soon as I get back to Montclair." Kevin scribbled his name and number on the card and pushed it across the counter.

He gave me a big smile as we headed toward the door. I smiled back, but I couldn't help but feel a little sad that Kevin would never save up enough money to buy those DVDs.

CHAPTER 20

While I waited for Kevin to arrive on the boardwalk with his cow suit, my skin tingled with excitement. I'd decided to do something different. Something I never would have done before the time loop.

A seagull dive-bombed a stale french fry as Kevin came up behind me. As always, he analyzed the man and woman and asked me if I wanted to put on the suit. That day I said, "Yes."

I stumbled as my sandal caught on the fabric. Once

I got my footing, I looked up at him and asked, "What does a cow say when she trips?"

"I don't know?"

"Moops!"

Kevin yelled, "Moops! Moops!" as he pretended to trip. Then the two of us laughed so hard that we had to stop ourselves from falling off the boardwalk into the sand.

Once I pulled on the hood with the ears, I posed like a fashion model with my hand on my hip.

"I've got to get some footage of this," Kevin said. He held up his camera and shouted, "Lights, camera, action!"

It was surprisingly fun walking down the boardwalk in costume. A little boy waved and smiled—as if I were a celebrity. Or maybe he thought I would give him a free sample of chicken, like that cow at the mall food court.

Some people made sure they kept their distance—as if I had some type of disease. Still, it was fun to watch people's reactions as I paraded along the boardwalk. I stopped and turned to Kevin. "I'm beginning to like this *moo-squerade*."

"It's cool to do something different once in a while," he said. "Isn't it?"

I bumped him with my hindquarter. "You don't know the half-and-half of it."

As I tapped the golf ball once and sent it straight to the Humpty Dumpty hole, it struck me how much I was changing when it came to sports and art, while everything else stayed the same.

"Hey, what's going on?" Kevin said. "You always complain you're not good at sports."

"Beginner's luck." The truth was that after all the practice, I'd figured out the trick of striking the ball a certain way, depending on which hole I was at.

Day after day, as my score improved, I realized how much Kevin did not like to lose at mini golf. After all, he was the one with the expertise. But I was playing as well as he was. Sometimes better.

I tried to stop myself from hitting the ball in the precise place or tapping it just the right amount, but I was really enjoying winning.

One day while watching Kevin struggle to get the ball past the paddles of the windmill, I felt a pang of guilt.

Then, suddenly, I had a great idea.

CHAPTER 21

The next morning, I crept into the living room early and inched open the top drawer of Dad's desk, where he kept his wallet. My pulse pounded as I ran my fingers across the smooth, black leather.

I reached into the dollars compartment and flipped through the bills: two fifties, a twenty, and a ten. Pressing my lips together, I held my breath and pulled out a fifty and a twenty.

My hands felt sweaty. I'd never stolen anything in my life.

But it wasn't really stealing. Was it?

I was just borrowing the money. I knew my father wouldn't touch his wallet all day. The next morning, his money would be back inside. He'd never know I took it.

I slipped the bills into my backpack and continued the day as if nothing unusual had happened.

Still, all morning long, I felt an excitement that I'd never experienced before. Was it because I was planning to surprise Kevin? Or that I'd gotten away with stealing?

During breakfast, while Kevin told me once again about his latest movie idea, I secretly plotted how I would get away from him.

I waited until he went home for the cow suit, knowing I had exactly twenty-two minutes until he came back. As soon as he was out of sight, I raced to the store.

"How may I help you?" Mr. Sidhu asked in his usual cheery voice.

"You know that DVD set that my friend Kevin has been looking at?"

"Of course," he said, reaching behind the counter. "Your friend has very good taste."

The DVDs were wrapped in plastic, so all I could

see was the movie on top: *The Colossus of New York.* "You're sure this is what he wanted?" I asked.

"Oh yes. These are four movies made many years ago. In the fifties. *Invasion of the Body Snatchers, The Day the Earth Stood Still, The Blob,* and this one." He pointed to the picture on the top DVD. There was a scary robot, a bunch of screaming people, and New York City in the background. Kevin would love it. And he'd finally get to see the beginning of that movie he'd been watching on TV.

I grabbed my wallet from my backpack and pulled out two bills. Mr. Sidhu's eyebrows came together. A wayward curl of black hair dangled in the middle of his forehead. "So, you are buying this for your friend as a gift?"

"Yes."

"This is a very expensive gift."

"Uh, well, I've been saving my money for it. I want to surprise Kevin."

Mr. Sidhu held the fifty up to the light and ran a marker across the front. "I must make sure any bill over twenty is not counterfeit," he said matter-of-factly.

"Unfortunately, there are many dishonest people in this world."

I looked down and swallowed hard. Had he emphasized the word "dishonest," or was it my imagination?

"I am sorry I do not have wrapping paper," Mr. Sidhu said.

"It's okay," I answered. "It's not Kevin's birthday or anything." The musty old book smell in the shop had gone from soothing to suffocating. The heel of my right foot bounced, and I couldn't make it stop.

Mr. Sidhu pulled a plastic bag out from under the counter and then slipped the DVDs inside. It felt like he was doing everything in slow motion.

"This is a fine gift," Mr. Sidhu said. "You are a very generous friend."

Could he tell I was lying about saving the money? I'd heard people do weird things with their eyes when they aren't telling the truth. Walking toward the exit, I tried to steady my eyeballs. I looked back over my shoulder, half expecting Mr. Sidhu to call the police as I opened the door. But he just waved and said, "I hope your friend enjoys the movies."

I took a huge breath of fresh air and shouted, "Thanks. I'm sure he will."

I sprinted back to where I was supposed to meet Kevin and tried to shake off the slithery feeling running through my veins.

As I watched him bound toward me in his cow suit, I forgot about everything. I couldn't wait to give him the gift. I pretended to be surprised as I listened to his cow facts and his theory about the cow suit personality test. But as soon as he finished, I whipped the DVDs out of my backpack and handed them to him.

His eyes widened. "What? Where did you get these?"

"At the store, of course."

"But where did you get the money? They're so expensive."

"Um, they went on sale." Another lie. I was getting good at it.

Kevin examined the DVDs. "This is so cool. Thanks!" He looked at me. "But we have to watch them together. Once we leave the shore, you can come to my house and we'll have a movie marathon."

"Yeah . . . that'll be great." I gave a weak smile,

knowing we'd never be able to watch all those movies together. The next morning they'd be back in the store, sitting on the shelf behind Mr. Sidhu.

A lump rose in my throat as I looked at Kevin's face, full of anticipation. I felt like a piece of fruit that was rotten on the inside, but still smooth and perfect on the outside.

CHAPTER 22

Once we got back from Atlantic City, instead of turning on the TV, Kevin pulled out one of his new DVDs. "C'mon," he said, setting his laptop on the kitchen table. "We can catch *The Colossus of New York* before dinner. He slipped the DVD into the slot and dragged two chairs together. Sitting next to him, I tried to contain my secret joy that I didn't have to watch the end of *The Day the Earth Stood Still* for the gazillionth time.

The smell of ragout and rosemary surrounded us. The movie was a sad one, about a man who got hit by a car and died. His father, a famous brain surgeon, operated and put his son's brain into a robot. But the robot turned bad and started terrorizing people.

Just as the robot was using his X-ray eyes to kill someone, Mr. Damico came into the kitchen. "Ah," he said, "*The Colossus of New York.* I saw that one when I was about your age. Scary, isn't it?"

"No way," Kevin said. "It's cool."

Mr. Damico laughed. "I guess it's cool. It's kind of a fifties version of *Frankenstein*."

Kevin paused the DVD. "What do you mean?"

Mr. Damico sat across from us. "Well, the brain surgeon father in the movie is just like Dr. Frankenstein. He starts off with good intentions but, instead, creates a monster."

"What are his good intentions?" Kevin asked.

"I suppose both stories have to do with finding the secret to immortality."

The second Mr. Damico finished, I blurted, without thinking, "But isn't that a good thing?"

Mr. Damico shook his head. "It never seems to work out. It's like they used to say in that old margarine commercial: 'It's not nice to fool Mother Nature.'"

Kevin gave a puzzled look. "What does that have to do with margarine?"

Mr. Damico shrugged. "I can't remember. But that phrase always stuck with me."

It stuck with me, too—all through the movie and dinner. By the time Kevin wanted me to play Scrabble, my mind was as mixed up as the tiles Kevin poured out onto the table. Still, I picked the same ones I did every night. I'd memorized everyone's letters as well as the words they'd put down. And I'd secretly researched tons of words on the Internet so I could figure out how to get the most points. I knew it was cheating. But it was just a game. It wasn't hurting anyone. Right?

So when Kevin put the letters *M, R, O, N* next to the letter *O* that was already on the board, I was ready. I scrunched up my face as if I were concentrating really hard, and then placed my *O, X,* and *Y* before the word "MORON." "Yes! Forty-two points!" I shouted.

"Oxymoron?" Kevin said. "How did you know how to spell that?"

"I looked it up."

"What?" he said. "When? You've been sitting here the whole time."

"Uh, I mean I looked it up once in school—when we studied poetry. It's when you put two words together that contradict each other."

"She's right, son," Mr. Damico said. "She's gotten us good."

I looked over at Mr. Damico and announced with authority, "Shakespeare uses it a lot. Like in *Romeo and Juliet*, when Romeo says, 'O brawling love! O loving hate!'"

Mr. Damico stroked his chin. "That's very impressive, Haleigh."

I felt a little guilty for trying to out-trivia Mr. Damico but thanked him anyway.

Kevin gave a baffled look, mixed with some frustration because I'd gotten so many points. "How can hate be loving?"

I shrugged and looked around the table for someone else to answer.

G-Mags chimed in from the couch, "When you get to be my age, you realize such contradictions are everywhere—wise fools, poor little rich girls . . ."

Kevin was quiet for a minute. "I've got one! The living dead—you know, like zombies."

Mrs. Damico laughed and said, "Leave it to Kevin to bring science fiction movies into it."

I could tell that made Kevin feel better. We continued with the game until it was time for me to go.

On the porch, I gave G-Mags the usual hug before leaving. And I smiled when she told me to come back in the morning, like she did every night.

But as I walked away with Dad, I couldn't get the words "living dead" out of my mind.

CHAPTER 23

That night, I lay in bed thinking about pizza and how I might never again get a slice at Chris's Place. Mom, Dad, and I would go there every Sunday night. When Chris would see us coming, he'd throw the sausage and pepperoni on the half for Dad and shove the pizza in the oven before we were even in our seats. I'd never realized how special those nights were. Or how much I'd miss them.

I took another glimpse of the painting on my desk. Up until then, I'd told myself I'd made the perfect wish. But I was starting to wonder.

When I heard Mom's footsteps, I jumped off the bed and started packing.

"All set for tomorrow?" she asked, entering my room.

I threw a shirt in my suitcase and nodded. Before I'd found the paint set, I never lied. At least, hardly ever. There was that time I'd told Abbey her new dress was pretty—even though I didn't like the shade of red. But that hadn't been a bad lie. Ever since the time loop started, I'd been lying to everyone. I felt like something inside me was shriveling up, like a seed with no water.

I wanted to tell the truth, but if I did, who would believe that we were all repeating the same day over and over? I wasn't even sure if it was happening only here at the shore. Or in all of New Jersey. Or, maybe, all over the world.

Were artists everywhere doing the same sketches over and over again every day? Just like I was.

"I'll give you a hand," Mom said. She picked up my sketchpad off the floor. "Did you do any drawings today?"

"A few."

"I'd love to see what you've done."

I flipped the cover and showed Mom some of the sketches I'd made earlier that day of Kevin and G-Mags.

She put her hand to her chest. "Oh my!" she exclaimed.

I dropped the pad and turned to her. "What is it? Are you okay?"

"These drawings. They're beautiful."

"Mom, you scared me!"

"Why have you been hiding them?"

"Uh, I don't know . . . to surprise you?" I really did hate lying to her.

"I knew you'd been practicing, but I had no idea how much you'd improved this summer." Her eyes got shiny.

"What's wrong?"

"I can't believe how lucky I am to have a daughter with this much talent. This drawing of Kevin . . . look at those details . . . just beautiful." She stroked my hair. "And you haven't even started lessons with your new art teacher yet."

My heart glowed inside me. "So you think he'll like these?"

"He'd be crazy not to."

Before the time loop, Mom and I talked about art all the time. Saturdays were our special day together. Mom would make chocolate chip pancakes and we'd stay in our pajamas till noon. But there were no more Saturdays. No more Sundays, either. When I thought about it, my chest felt hollow.

I gestured to the book in Mom's hand, the one with the picture of van Gogh's famous painting *The Starry Night* on the cover. "Tell me more about van Gogh."

"Let's see," she said. "Here's a little-known fact: in Holland, they pronounce his name *van Hauck*." She said it like there was something stuck in the back of her throat and she was trying to cough it up.

"Really?" I imitated her pronunciation—"van *Houck*"—and had to swallow several times before I could talk again. "Tell me more," I said, "about his art."

She pointed to the painting on the book cover. "Here you can see van Gogh made the swirls in the clouds look like a yin-yang symbol."

"Yin-yang? What's that?"

"It's a symbol found in Eastern religions. It represents what we think of as opposite forces. Like male and female, destruction and creation, dark and—"

"But why would van Gogh put that symbol in the middle of the painting?"

"No one will ever know. That's the beauty of art. Perhaps it had something to do with the necessity of opposing forces: shadows can't exist without light. We wouldn't know something was sweet if we never tasted something bitter."

"So, it's like an oxymoron?"

"Yes, sort of. Vincent van Gogh was a troubled soul. He might have been suggesting something about accepting both the good and bad aspects of life."

"But what if we didn't have to accept the bad?" I asked.

"What do you mean?"

"What if we could live in paradise, like the story of Adam and Eve before the apple—with nothing terrible ever happening?"

"I guess it would be nice for a while, but after too long it might be like eating dessert all the time."

"What's wrong with that?"

Mom laughed and grabbed my hand. "Right now, absolutely nothing. In fact, how about we share that cannoli in the refrigerator?"

"Oops." I let go of her hand.

"What is it?"

"I'm sorry. I ate it already . . . but don't worry. I'll save it for you tomorrow night."

"Tomorrow?"

"Uh, I mean, maybe tomorrow G-Mags can make more for us to take home."

Mom patted her stomach. "It's okay. It probably wouldn't have been good for me to eat it now anyway. I've been having a lot of indigestion these days." She gave me a kiss on the head. "See you tomorrow morning."

"Yup. See you tomor—uh . . . in the morning."

CHAPTER 24

The next day when I was filling the bucket with water, I studied the two girls walking by. When they laughed at the stegosaurus, I kind of understood. Even though I wasn't changing on the outside, I felt like I might be different on the inside—because I didn't feel mad at them anymore. I kind of wanted to become like them: older, more confident.

And then it hit me: I'd never *become* anything. Not an artist, not a professor like Mom and Dad, not anything. There at the shore, I'd always just *be*. I'd never *become*.

I reminded myself it was a good thing. The future

could be so much worse: G-Mags could die. Kevin and I could drift apart. And who knew what other bad things could happen to me or Mom or Dad or any of us?

I watched Mateo and how excited he was, working side by side with Kevin. I figured he, more than anyone, would want a never-ending summer.

Back at the stegosaurus, I grabbed a handful of sand. "Hey, guys, I have a question: What if you could live the same day over and over—without growing older or getting sick or anything bad happening, ever?"

Mateo answered right away. "Depends on what day you're talking about."

"What day?" I was surprised he hadn't just answered *yes*.

"Yeah, like maybe if it was my birthday, and I was having a party, and I got some really cool presents. I wouldn't mind living that day over and over again."

Kevin laughed and gave Mateo a fist bump. "Good answer."

I ignored them and continued, "What if it was *this* day?"

Mateo shook his head. "No way. I mean it's an okay day, but nothing special."

I gestured to Kevin. "What about you?"

He shook his head. "Even though today's been a pretty good day so far, there's a lot of stuff I'd miss."

"Like what?"

"Like seeing my brother again."

"What else?"

"Well, I've been hoping they'd make another Iron Man movie—I'd like to see that. And I'd really like to get some footage of a werewolf. And—"

"But what if living the same day over and over was preventing some kind of tragedy?"

"That could be cool," Kevin said. "I saw this movie about a guy who keeps living the same train trip over and over so he can find the bomber on the train, but . . . I still think I'd probably want to keep time moving." Kevin grabbed a handful of sand and let it sift through his fingers. "What about you? You wouldn't want to live the same day over and over again, would you?"

I shook my head, avoiding Kevin's eyes. "No, I guess not."

And for the first time since I'd used the magic paints, I realized I might have made a huge mistake.

CHAPTER 25

I couldn't shake the feeling that even though I was spending every day with Kevin, I was growing away from him—and everyone else, including Mom. So that afternoon, I decided to fake sickness and stay home instead of going to Atlantic City.

As soon as Mom was done planting her seeds, she sat on the couch with her laptop, and I curled up beside her.

"Feeling better?" she asked.

"A little. But . . . I've been thinking about things."

"Like what?"

"Dad taught me about Einstein, so I've been reading more about time and space."

"That's an awfully serious thing to be thinking about, particularly during summer vacation." Mom put her arm around me. "Tell me what you learned."

"One thing I read was about how the Earth gains a few minutes every century. In the time of the dinosaurs, there were only twenty-three hours in a day. And millions of years from now, a day will be twenty-five hours."

"Interesting," Mom said. "I guess we won't be around to see that twenty-five-hour day, which is probably a good thing."

"Why?"

"These days, I'm exhausted by eight o'clock at night. I can't imagine having to work an extra hour." She smiled. "Especially if I were more than a million years old."

"I guess you're right," I said. "It would be great if we never had to get older, wouldn't it?"

Mom squeezed my shoulder. "As much as I'd love for you to stay my little girl forever, I don't think I'd like that."

"But isn't this a great summer? Wouldn't you want it to last forever?"

Mom closed her laptop. "I do love being here at the shore with you and your father. And I do like the idea of never getting wrinkles or arthritis . . . but there are a few reasons why I wouldn't want to keep living this day over and over."

"Like what?"

She picked up a stack of paper next to her on the couch. "I'd love to finish all this work on van Gogh, so I can finally publish my book."

"But what if you didn't know that you'd never finish. Isn't doing the research fun enough?"

"Sure it is, but I'd love the satisfaction of seeing a finished book and having people enjoy it. Do you know that van Gogh created more than two thousand works of art and only sold one painting in his lifetime?"

"Wow! Two thousand! No wonder he was such a good artist—he got a lot of practice."

"Can you imagine doing all that work and never knowing how the world appreciated it?" Mom said. "He never had any idea how many people would admire his work in museums all over the world."

I nodded, thinking about how good my drawings were getting—and only Mom had seen them. "That *is* sad."

Mom's eyes turned even more serious. "It's a shame he couldn't have known the future. Maybe he would have been happier. And maybe he wouldn't have taken his own life at such a young age. We'll never know."

I thought about how van Gogh didn't know his future and how, if the time loop continued, I would never know mine. Would I be a famous artist, like van Gogh? Or an art history professor, like Mom? Then I thought of all the bad things that could happen in the future, and my head started to hurt.

"Are you okay?" Mom asked.

"Yes. But you're sure you wouldn't want this summer to last forever?"

"I don't have that choice. But even if I did, this morning when I woke up, I wasn't feeling too well." Mom put her hand on her stomach. "I would hate for that to happen every day of my life."

I hadn't really noticed, but after Mom mentioned it, I remembered she'd been in the bathroom for a long time. My own stomach tightened, and I wondered if

Mom was sick. I studied her face. Had she always had those dark circles under her eyes? How could I have been so selfish not to notice what was going on with my own mother?

As soon as she got up from the couch, I took over the laptop and typed in her symptoms: *stomach problems and tired eyes.* A list of possible illnesses popped up: everything from lactose intolerance to mononucleosis to things so terrible I didn't even want to think about them.

I knew it wasn't lactose intolerance. Mom would have been sick before summer—ice cream is one of her favorite desserts. Weight loss was another symptom, and earlier that day she'd complained her pants were getting tight.

I clicked on the next disease. If Mom had mononucleosis, she'd have other signs, like a fever or a sore throat.

I scrolled through the list. When I got to the end and read the symptoms on the last page, I gasped.

Mom was having a baby!

CHAPTER 26

That night, I stared at the painting and wondered how I could have been so selfish when I made my wish. I'd thought only of myself and about how much I wanted things to stay the same. But what about Mom? All summer long she'd been tired and sick, and I never even noticed.

And G-Mags: even though she said her dizzy spells were nothing, who knows how she was when we weren't there. Maybe she felt sick too, but didn't want to worry everyone.

I had to do something!

After retrieving the yellow box from my closet, I studied the words: *Paint your heart's desire.*

Maybe if I did another painting, I could undo the first one. I had more oil paint. But not another canvas. Would the paints work on paper?

I ripped two sheets from my sketchpad. On one page, I painted a calendar with numbers that went all the way to the end of the year. I figured that would get time moving again.

On the second sheet, I painted the word "G-Mags." I held up the two pages, squeezed my eyes shut, and wished for G-Mags to be okay and for time to keep moving.

I hurried to bed and crossed all my fingers and toes, hoping my plan worked.

But when the doorbell rang a little while later, that hope dissolved like a wave hitting a sand castle.

CHAPTER 27

Although my plan with the paints hadn't worked, I was determined to figure out how to get time moving. As I headed toward Mr. Sidhu's store, the seagulls squawked and flapped around me with urgency. Was it because they were hungry for the breakfast scraps scattered along the boardwalk? Or did they have some special kind of bird ESP that made them aware of the time loop? I'd heard that animals could sometimes tell when a hurricane or tsunami was coming, way before humans had any idea. Were these seagulls psychic?

As I passed the early-morning crowd doing their tai chi exercises on the beach, the smell of waffles sailed by. My stomach growled. I'd gotten up extra early so I could quiz Mr. Sidhu before meeting Kevin for breakfast. Mr. Sidhu had read all kinds of books. Maybe he could help me figure out how to stop the time loop.

The bell above me jingled as I pulled the door open. As usual, Mr. Sidhu was reading the book with the spaceship on the cover. He looked up. "Good morning. You are early today? Yes?" I nodded as he added, "How may I help you?" His voice was as cheery as always. How would he feel if he knew he'd been flipping through the same pages in the same book for weeks and weeks?

I strolled up to the counter. "I know you've read a lot of science fiction, and I was wondering if you've ever read a story about a time loop."

Mr. Sidhu put his book facedown on the counter. "I thought you liked mystery novels. Your friend is the fan of science fiction. No?"

"Well, yes, he is," I said. "But he told me I would like a particular story he read—about a time loop. It sounded interesting. He couldn't remember the end, so I thought I'd read it and find out." *More lies.*

"Much of science fiction is about time travel. What is the name of the story?"

"It's called '12:01 P.M.'"

"Ah yes, that is a classic."

"So, you know it? Can you tell me what happens at the end?"

"Do you really want to know? I do not want to spoil it for you."

"Yes. Yes. I want to know!"

Mr. Sidhu's dark eyebrows came together. "Let me see. At the end of the story, the man has a heart attack, and he knows he is dying. He thinks the time loop will be over because of his death. But he is wrong. As soon as the clock hits one minute after one o'clock, it bounces back one hour. And the man is alive again."

"So he's still in the time loop? That's a terrible ending!"

Mr. Sidhu smiled. "Well then, you will be happy to know the author wrote another story with the same character. It is called '12:02 P.M.'"

"What happens in that story?"

Mr. Sidhu thought for a minute. "The man thinks he has figured out the solution to his problem. If he throws himself out of a window, he will be able to get time moving again."

"What?" I rocked back on my heels and almost fell. "He jumps out a window?"

"Yes. That is the end of the story."

The backs of my legs tingled just thinking about it. But I didn't think leaping out a window had anything to do with the time loop I was in. "Do you know of any other stories that have to do with a time loop?" I asked. "Maybe that involve paints?"

Mr. Sidhu hesitated. "It is not exactly about a time loop. But I know of a famous book about a man who wishes on a painting of himself. After that, the portrait grows old, and the man stays young."

"What happens at the end?"

"I believe the artist stabs the painting with a knife."

"Then what happens?" I held my breath, waiting to hear the answer.

Mr. Sidhu frowned. "I am not sure I should tell you—it is a little gruesome."

"Please, tell me. Tell me!"

"The portrait changes back to being the man when he was young again and—"

"The man? What happens to the man?"

"He withers away."

"Withers?" I felt like there was a wad of saltwater taffy stuck in my throat.

Mr. Sidhu nodded and looked around. "I do not think I have a copy of that book."

"That's okay," I said, heading out to the boardwalk.

I checked my reflection in the glass door on the way out. I had to find out where those paints came from—before I ended up like that guy in the book.

CHAPTER 28

After leaving Mr. Sidhu's shop, I texted Kevin and told him I'd wait for him at Annie's. I had to get time moving again. And that meant I had to find the directions to the paints. But where were they? And how could I find them if I didn't know where the paints came from?

I flashed back to when I'd first seen the yellow box on the night of the first last day. It hadn't been in my backpack when I left the house that morning. That meant someone had to have given me the box at some point during that day.

But who?

And why?

I decided to make a list of people and places I'd seen that first day. I grabbed my pencil and sketchpad from my backpack and began writing frantically:

1. *Met Kevin on boardwalk and went to Annie's for breakfast.*
2. *Looked at Serena's sketches.*
3. *Went to Mr. Sidhu's store with Kevin.*
4. *Ate Italian ice with Kevin on boardwalk.*
5. *Swam and sculpted stegosaurus with Kevin and Mateo on beach.*
6. *Waited while Kevin went to get cow suit.*
7. *Made cannolis with Kevin and G-Mags.*
8. *Went home to change.*
9. *Went to Atlantic City.*
    - A. *Observed gamblers.*
    - B. *Ate tacos.*
    - C. *Shopped for souvenirs.*
    - D. *Watched magic show.*
    - E. *Played mini golf.*
10. *Had dinner with Kevin's family.*

I studied the list. Did I have enough information to solve this mystery by myself?

There was one person who could help me: Kevin. He paid attention to everything—especially when he was filming.

But did I dare tell him about the painting? What would I say? *Hey, guess what? I found a set of paints in my backpack, and when I used them it caused a monumental rift in the space-time continuum—just like those movies you love so much.*

No. He'd never believe me.

Still, I knew if anyone could help me solve the mystery, it was Kevin.

I looked up from the list as he strolled in, wearing that same shirt with Captain America on it. As he slipped into the booth, I made a split-second decision. I took a deep breath and whispered at rapid speed, "Listen, I have something really important to tell you. You may not believe me. But you've got to help me. No matter what. Promise?"

Kevin's eyes widened. "What is it? Are you okay? Did something happen to you?"

"No. Well, yes. Sort of. Just tell me you'll believe

what I say—even though it'll sound impossible."

Kevin's expression changed, and it reminded me of the look on his face every night when he came through the door. "Of course I'll believe you. You know you can count on me for *anything*."

The way he said "anything" made me believe him with my whole heart. "Okay, I'm going to talk fast because we don't have a lot of time."

"You're scaring me," Kevin said.

"Don't be scared. Just listen." The words flew from my mouth, almost at the speed of light.

Kevin's eyes were glued to mine as I spoke. His expression remained serious.

But the second I finished, he broke into a huge grin. "You had me going there for a while."

I'd expected that might happen. "Honest," I said. "I've done enough research to know we can't explain everything about space and time. And I'm telling the truth."

"Sure you are." He laughed and shook his head.

I had to do something to make him believe me. As soon as I spotted Annie walking our way, I ripped a small piece of paper off the bottom of the list and wrote on it. I folded it into a tiny square, slid it across the table, and demanded, "Don't open this until Annie leaves."

Kevin ordered the usual and I asked for a bowl of banana nut granola. We had our everyday conversation with Annie. Then her eyes welled up just before Joey flipped the pancake, and it landed on the floor.

As soon as Annie left, I pointed to the folded square. "Go ahead, open it."

Kevin unfolded the note and read what I'd written: *Splat! Joey just dropped a pancake on the floor.* Kevin looked puzzled at first, but then smiled. "That was a pretty good trick."

"Trick? What do you mean?"

"You were here before me. You must have made a deal with Joey to drop the pancake."

"No. No. I didn't talk to Joey at all. Go ask him. I knew it would happen because it happens every day. Because *every day is the same.*"

Kevin put the note on the table. "Even if you didn't talk to Joey, it's not that surprising that he dropped the pancake. He is kind of clumsy. Remember that time he knocked the wooden ark full of muffins off the counter?"

"Okay, you have a point."

Kevin nodded. "Let's see if you can tell me something else that'll happen."

I rattled off a list of events, starting with Mateo's joke from the Popsicle stick and everything after that, including building the stegosaurus and helping G-Mags cook.

"I guess those things might happen," Kevin said with a wrinkled brow. "But now that you've put them into my head, we'll probably do all those things."

"What about Mateo's joke?"

"You could have planted the Popsicle stick so he'd find it."

"Why would I go to all that trouble?"

Kevin's eyes narrowed. "That's what I can't figure out. So far, none of this makes sense."

"Okay, let me give you more proof. Later, you're going to tell me you have to go back home to get something to surprise me."

Kevin straightened up in his seat.

"And then you're going to show up on the boardwalk wearing a cow suit."

Kevin's mouth fell open. "I . . . I talked to my mom

before I came here. She was cleaning out the house and told me she found my cow suit. I told her she should bring it when they come later today."

I gave a tentative smile. "See. How could I have known that?"

Kevin shook his head. "This is crazy."

"No crazier than all those sci-fi films you love. Look at how many things in those old movies have come true: robots that clean your house, wristwatches that you talk to, computers that can do almost anything."

"But that's not magic. That's science."

"Maybe this is too. I don't know. All I know is that we have to stop it."

"How?"

"I have to find out where the paints came from. Will you help me?"

He looked at me with a confused expression. I could tell he still thought I was joking, and I knew there was one thing I could say that would convince him I wasn't.

I hesitated. "There's something I didn't mention."

"What is it?"

"At the end of the day . . . something bad happens."

"Go on."

I lowered my eyes and shook my head. "I can't say it."

"C'mon," Kevin said. "You have to tell me."

Without looking up, I whispered, "It's G-Mags."

"What happens to her?"

"She . . . she has a stroke."

"So are you saying that if I help you find out who gave you the paints, we can fix things, and she'll be okay? She won't have a stroke?"

I shake my head. "No."

"No? Then why are you telling me this?"

"In the beginning, I tried to warn her. I really did. I thought maybe that was why this happened. So I could prevent her from having it, but . . ."

He leaned across the table. "But what?"

"But I could never stop it from happening."

Kevin put his head in his hands for a few seconds and then looked up. His face was red. "What's going on?" He looked around. "Is someone making you do this?"

"No. I'm telling you the truth."

"It's impossible."

"I know. I know it's crazy. But I swear it's true."

"Then what happens afterward?"

"The ambulance takes her to the hospital."

"Then what?"

"I don't know. In the morning, everything's always the same as the day before."

Kevin grabbed his backpack and raced out of Annie's. I threw some money on the table and followed him, yelling, "I'm sorry. I'm sorry."

When I finally caught up to him, he turned to me with hurt in his eyes. "Do you think you're funny—trying to fool me? I might have gone along with the joke, but I can't believe you took it this far." His voice cracked. "I can't believe you brought G-Mags into it."

"You have to believe me. I would never joke about something like that. It's true."

"It can't be. There's no such thing as magic."

I sped up to keep pace with him. "I thought so too. But I know what's been happening to me. And there's no other explanation."

He stopped to face me. "Are you really telling me the truth? Do you swear that if you're lying, you'll rip up every drawing in your sketchbook?"

"I swear," I said. "I'll destroy it all."

He was quiet for a few seconds and then took a deep

breath. "I know how much those sketches mean to you. So, even if what you're saying is impossible, even if it's not true at all, you must believe it's true."

"I do."

"Then shouldn't you have been able to help G-Mags?"

"Believe me, I tried. In the beginning I told your parents to call 911 when she got her first dizzy spell, but no one would listen. They thought I was overreacting. Then I looked up stroke prevention online to see if there was something I could do. I even called an ambulance to the house a bunch of times. But nothing I did could prevent it from happening."

"Maybe you didn't try hard enough." There was a hint of anger in his voice.

"I'm sorry," I said. "But if there's one thing I've figured out all these weeks, it's that some things are meant to be. I've been able to change certain things, like what I eat or whether I go with you to Atlantic City. But there are some things I just can't change. And G-Mags having a stroke is one of them."

"I still don't believe you!"

"Okay, even if I'm lying, don't you think it's worth

pretending to believe me? To try and save G-Mags?"

"Maybe. I don't know." He collapsed onto a nearby bench. "You've got me so confused."

"I'm sorry. I didn't mean to."

He rubbed his temples over and over. "Even if you *are* telling the truth? What can I do?"

"I don't know."

"I have to do something to try and save her. Make her go to the hospital. *Something*."

"Maybe she'll listen to you," I said. "I don't know. Go home and see. I'll wait for you here on the boardwalk."

CHAPTER 29

While Kevin was away, I ran home and stuffed the box of paints in my backpack. When I returned to the bench, I waited for almost an hour, wondering if I'd done the right thing, wondering if Kevin would come back. I knew no matter what, he'd forget all of it the next morning, but I couldn't stand the thought of him hating me, even for just one day.

I tried to take my mind off things by watching people cruise along the boardwalk.

Two little kids giggled as frozen custard dripped

down their cones. The parents, holding large cinnamon elephant ears, urged the boy and girl to hurry up.

Weeks ago, my mouth would have watered at the sight. But Mom was right. Dessert was no fun when you could eat it all the time.

I was just about to give up on Kevin when I spotted him heading slowly toward me. His shoulders were slumped. "She didn't believe it," he said, sitting beside me on the bench. "I tried to get her to call the doctor. But she said she felt fine."

"I'm sorry."

"It isn't your fault."

I nodded, but deep down I felt like it was.

"You said the same thing happens to her every night? It must be so scary for her."

"For you, too," I said, remembering the look on his face each night. "There's something else I haven't told you."

"About G-Mags?"

"No, about my mom."

"Does something happen to her, too?"

"Not today. But . . ."

"But what? Tell me."

"I'm pretty sure she's having a baby."

"Wow, really? How do you know?"

"She has all the symptoms: she sleeps a lot, she's making all of us eat healthier, and she's extra crazy when it comes to germs."

"You're sure she's not just sick?"

"I don't think so—except for morning sickness and stuff like that. So, you see why I have to get us out of this time loop? If I don't, my new brother or sister will never be born."

"And I'll never see Michael again? Or grow up and go to college?"

"Right."

"Or finish my movie?"

I shook my head. "You've been filming the same thing for weeks and weeks."

"But what will happen to G-Mags if time moves forward?"

I hugged my backpack to my chest and whispered, "I don't know."

"Is there a chance we can save her?"

"Maybe."

Kevin stared out at the beach for a long while, as

if he were doing a complicated math problem in his head. Finally, he looked at me and said, "I'm still not sure I believe you. But since you believe it, I'll help you. Show me the paints."

I pulled the yellow box from my backpack and opened the flap. "Have you ever seen anything like this before?"

Kevin reached for one of the tubes and shook his head. "They look really old."

"I know."

"Why would someone give you a paint set and not even tell you they gave it to you?"

"That's what I want to know." I took out the list I'd shown him earlier.

"These are all the places we went. I need you to help me figure out where I might have left my backpack on that first day. If I find out who gave them to me, maybe I can discover how they work. And I can undo what happened."

Kevin looked at the list. "I remember doing some of these things—we've done most of them every day. But why can't I remember building a stegosaurus or making cannolis or going to Atlantic City?"

"Because, technically, you didn't do them yet."

"Wait a minute!" Kevin jumped up from the bench. "There's this theory I read about. I thought it was only in science fiction. But maybe it's real."

"What is it? Tell me!"

"It's called the many-worlds theory. Some scientists think that for each minute, more than one possible future exists. And all these futures can be happening at the same time."

"What would that have to do with what's happening to me?"

"Maybe we're living in parallel universes. Maybe it's only in *your* universe where you're living the same day over and over—because of the painting. But in *my* universe, summer's over, and we're already back in school."

"But how do I get time moving again? I don't want to stay trapped in August twenty-sixth in any universe."

"I don't know," Kevin said. "I'm not sure what to believe or how this is possible. But if you're telling the truth, we've got to do something." He waved the paint box in the air. "You're sure it has something to do with these?"

I nodded and breathed a grateful sigh that he believed me.

"So how do we find out where they came from?"

I looked up at him. "I've been thinking . . . we need to go through this whole day with you filming it."

"But if you already have the paints, there won't be any film of the person sticking them into your backpack."

"I thought of that. But if I can study all the different people we came in contact with, maybe I'll get some clues about which one of them it could be." I took the list from Kevin and folded it. "We've got to go about our usual day, and then tonight, when we get back from Atlantic City, we'll look at your tape and see who looks suspicious."

Kevin fished out his video camera from his backpack. "Even if we're living in parallel universes, and my life is moving forward in the other one, I don't want to be stuck in time anywhere."

"So . . . you'll help me?"

"Sure, but we can't be too obvious about filming everyone." He hoisted his backpack onto one shoulder and swung it around to the front. Then he tucked the camera inside, just enough so the lens peeked out. "That should do it."

"Okay, then. Let's hurry. We've got to stay on schedule."

Kevin stood and turned the backpack my way. "Lights, camera, action!"

CHAPTER 30

When we got back from Atlantic City, Kevin and I stayed out on the porch to examine what he'd filmed. The smell of ragout and rosemary sailed our way as Kevin dragged two rocking chairs together. "Let's rewind the day," he said. "What happened before I met you at Annie's?" His voice sounded deep and official, like a TV detective. "Was anyone near you on the boardwalk?"

I shook my head as we sat. "No. And I had my backpack on my shoulder the whole time."

"What about when you got to Annie's?"

"I kept my backpack right next to me on the seat. No one could have slipped anything inside without me seeing it. Right?"

"I don't know," Kevin said. "What about when Joey dropped that pancake on the floor? Didn't we all turn to look? Could Annie have put the paints in your backpack on that first day, while no one was looking at her?"

"I think Annie was just as surprised as we were. Besides, that first day was the same as today. She was only holding a pencil and pad—and the pockets in her apron were way too small to hide anything."

"Okay," Kevin said. "Let's do this systematically. We need to cross things out one at a time."

I gave him the list and my colored pencils. Kevin balanced the paper on his knee and drew a red line through Number One. He took out his camera. "What about Serena? Have you noticed anything unusual about her?"

"No way. Even though I put her on the list, I don't think it's her."

"We can't rule out anybody—no matter how much you like them. Think about it. Serena's an artist. She must have lots of old paints lying around. And she knows you're an artist too. Maybe they were hers when she was your age, and she wanted to pass them on."

"But why wouldn't she tell me she was giving them to me?"

Kevin shrugged and pressed play. There was footage of the little girl squirming in the chair and Serena frowning under her huge hat. Kevin paused the tape. "Maybe she wanted to surprise you. C'mon. It makes perfect sense."

"I don't know . . . maybe." I tried to remember all those weeks ago when I first saw Serena painting the little girl with the polka-dot bow. Had I put my backpack down when I was admiring the sketches? I turned the camera to get a better view. "Does Serena seem suspicious to you?"

"She did tell us one of her ancestors was put to death after the Salem witch trials."

"What's that got to do with anything?"

Kevin shrugged. "Maybe she inherited some magic powers."

I shook my head. "I don't think so."

"You have to admit, she is kind of eccentric with those weird hats. And look at the one she's wearing. It's huge—she could have hidden anything under there." He rested the camera on the porch floor. "Give me the green pencil. We'll color-code the list. Strong suspects get a green star."

"Okay," I said. But I didn't really think Serena was a strong suspect.

"On to Number Three," Kevin said. "Mr. Sidhu's."

"Did you see anyone get close enough to me at the store?"

"It was crowded in there, but wouldn't you have felt it if someone slipped a box that big inside your backpack?"

"It's been so long, I can't remember that first time." Had there been anyone suspicious in the store? Or . . . what about Mr. Sidhu? "Show me the film."

I watched myself leafing through the mystery novels. Someone bumped into me, and I fell back against the counter. "Look! That happens every day. Maybe on that first day, somebody gave me the paints while I was trying to catch my balance."

Kevin rewound the tape. "I guess so. But Mr. Sidhu was the closest to your backpack. Why would he give them to you?"

"He could have seen me sketching on the boardwalk one morning when we first got to the shore and thought I would like them. Maybe he found the box mixed in with a bunch of used books and figured no one would want to buy used paints."

"You think?"

"It's possible. He's a very nice man. Remember how he said he'd give you first dibs on those DVDs you like? You should give him a green star too."

"Okay. Where was your backpack when we were on the boardwalk and the beach?"

"I had it when we got the Italian ices, but it was on my towel when we went for a swim. We asked that couple next to us to watch our stuff, and they didn't seem like people who would sneak paints into a kid's backpack. Did they?"

"I don't think so. But what kind of people *would* do that?"

"And why?" I added.

"That's a good question," Kevin said. "And one we haven't explored yet. What's the motive?"

"Motive?"

"Yeah, you know, on all those TV cop shows, they

talk about whether the criminal had the opportunity to do the crime and what their reason, or motive, for doing it was."

"You think a criminal gave me the paints?"

"Could be," Kevin said. "It's a pretty weird thing to do. And look what happened after you used them. It's kind of scary."

"I guess. But a criminal?" A chill ran through me, even though the thermometer on the porch read ninety degrees. "It's creepy thinking someone I may not even know went into my backpack."

"Hang on," Kevin said. "I didn't mean to scare you. Criminals don't *give* you things. They *steal* them, right?"

"That's it!" I jumped up from the chair.

"What?"

"Maybe someone stole the paints and then stashed them in my backpack when he—"

"Or she," Kevin said. "We haven't ruled out Serena."

"Okay. Or *she* was about to get caught."

"Hmm," Kevin said. "I suppose that's a possibility." He picked up the box and examined it. "Why would anyone want to steal these? They look like they're fifty years old."

"That's true." I pointed to the list. "We're getting off track. Where were we?" I sat back down.

"Number Five—the beach and the couple that was supposed to be watching our stuff."

"Let's look at the film you took of the stegosaurus. They might be in the background, and we can see if they look suspicious."

Kevin played the tape. First there was a close-up of the sand, then the stegosaurus, then Mateo and me, running down the beach. "Wait," Kevin said, rewinding a little. "There's the couple in the corner. Their eyes are totally shut. They weren't watching our stuff at all."

"Could someone have hidden the paints in my bag while they weren't looking?"

"Could be," Kevin said. "Or maybe someone at the beach got confused and thought your backpack was theirs."

I pointed to the pink hearts and yellow flowers I'd painted all over my backpack. "I don't think anyone could mistake this for theirs."

"You're right," Kevin said. "But we still can't rule out someone on the beach." He crossed out Number Four, since the bag never left my shoulder at the Italian ice stand, but drew a green star next to Number Five. "Okay, let's see, Number Six. Did anything weird happen while I was getting the cow suit?"

I shook my head.

"I didn't see anyone touch your backpack while we were here making cannolis." He drew red lines through Six and Seven. "Number Eight," Kevin said, suddenly getting a strange look on his face. "Could your parents have put them in your backpack when you went home?"

"Why would they do that?"

"To surprise you?"

I shook my head. "No way. Especially with Mom's germ phobia. If she found a box this old, she would have thrown it away and washed her hands with alcohol ten times."

"What about your dad?"

"Same thing."

"You're sure? I mean, they haven't told you yet about the baby. They're keeping one secret. Maybe they have another one."

"I get why they kept it a secret about Mom's pregnancy—she's been trying for years to have another baby. They probably didn't want me to get too excited until they knew for sure everything was okay."

"I'm sorry," Kevin said. "I didn't mean they were hiding things from you on purpose. I just thought maybe they wanted to distract you with the paints . . . you know, until they thought it was the right time to tell you."

"You could be right."

"So what should we do? Cross out or green star?"

I took a deep breath and whispered, "Green star."

"Okay. Moving on. We're up to Number Nine: Atlantic City. We can cross out *A* and *C*. There was no one near us when we were watching the gamblers or shopping for souvenirs." Kevin's eyes grew wide. "But what about that sketchy guy sitting behind you at the Mexican restaurant?"

"I guess it could be him."

"He was really strange," Kevin said. "And he was wearing a suit. Who wears a suit on the shore in summer? But . . ."

"But what?"

He played back some film from the restaurant. "Look. Dracula never went near your backpack."

"Wait a minute." My heart raced. "Yes! Yes, he did!"

CHAPTER 31

What?" Kevin said. "Watch the film—he wasn't near your backpack at all."

"Not today. But you don't remember that very first day when you blew the straw paper across the table. I missed, and it hit the man on the neck. After a while, he leaned down like he was looking for whatever hit him. He could have shoved the box in my backpack when he was bending over."

"Hmm. Another strong suspect," Kevin said. "What would his motive be?"

I thought for a minute. "If he's a writer, like we thought, he could have done it for a story."

"What do you mean?"

"Maybe he didn't know the paints were magic, but he put them in my backpack to see what I'd do with them. Remember, we kept seeing him at the hotel. He could have been watching us to find out what we'd do when I found the paints."

"Then what?"

"He'd have the beginning of a new novel—depending on what we did with them."

"But you didn't find them till you got home. Wouldn't he have tried to get you to open your backpack before we left the hotel?"

"I guess." My head was spinning with all these theories. "The paints are so old. He could have gotten a good deal on a bunch of them and put the boxes in a lot of kids' backpacks. Maybe some other kid found them first and the guy got his story idea without me."

"That is one weird hypothesis," Kevin said. "Maybe *you* should be a writer."

"I'm an artist. Not a writer. But if my theory is true, I am a little sad I didn't get to be in his book. I feel kind of sorry for him. He probably had no idea he was missing out on a story about magic."

All of a sudden, Kevin jumped out of the rocking chair and yelled, "Magic! Why didn't I think of this sooner!"

"Think of what?"

"Marty the magician. He had his hands right near your backpack when he pulled that scarf out."

"I thought you didn't believe in magic?"

"I don't. It had to be a trick. You know, sleight of hand."

Kevin pressed play again. "Look. I got a shot of him covering one hand with the other when he pulled out the scarf. That's how he does it. He gets you looking at one hand while he does something else with the other one."

"Why would Marty do a trick like that and not follow up on it? Wouldn't he have shown everyone how he put the box in there without anyone seeing it? It would be his moment of glory, right?"

Kevin paced across the porch. "I don't know. Maybe he got distracted by a customer—and we left the store." Kevin drew two green stars next to Marty's name. "He might be the most likely suspect so far. He had the opportunity to do it and he had a motive."

"I guess so, but I'm still going with my writer theory. Draw two stars next to him."

"All right. But we still need to finish with the list. What did we do next?"

"You went to tell your mom that we were going to play mini golf."

"That's right. And when I came back, your backpack was unzipped. That *proves* it was Marty."

"Are you sure? He's good with the cards and the scarves, but I can't believe he could hide a whole box of paints. And . . . wait a minute!" I narrowed my eyes at Kevin. "You came up from *behind* me and said my backpack was open. *You* could have put the paints in there!"

Kevin flinched as if I'd slapped him. "Why would I do that? And where would I have gotten the paints?"

"I don't know. Maybe your mom found them at home when she was cleaning out your stuff."

"Why wouldn't I tell you that I was giving them to you?"

"To surprise me?"

"With a set of old, used paints?"

I rocked back and forth at rapid speed. "I guess not."

"Besides," Kevin said, "I already know what I'm getting you for Christmas, and it isn't used."

Christmas? Had Kevin already been planning that far ahead? Why had I been so worried we wouldn't see each other after summer? It was like I'd been preparing for something before it even happened.

Mom once told me about this thing called the self-fulfilling prophecy, how sometimes if you think the worst is going to happen, it will—because you end up making it happen. Had I always drifted apart from my friends because I expected to? Was I the one who was really pulling away because I was afraid they'd do it first? Had I even done it with Abbey?

At that moment, I wanted more than ever for time to move forward. I *had* to find out who gave me the yellow box. I looked at Kevin's hurt face. "I know it wasn't you . . . maybe it was someone at mini golf."

"But you had the backpack with you the whole time."

"No! No, I didn't. You don't remember, but on that first day, the rickshaw driver swerved and knocked you down. I didn't get there in time to pull you out of the way, like I did today. He took me by surprise the first time, and when I ran to help you, I left my backpack on a bench at the last hole."

"It's weird I can't remember that," Kevin said. "Did I get hurt?"

"You skinned your knee."

"Why were you able to pull me away in time? But we can't save G-Mags?"

"I wondered that for a long time, but . . ." I looked away and rocked faster in the chair. "I think some things are just meant to be."

Kevin was quiet for a while, and I wasn't sure what to say. Finally, he looked up and drew a green star next to mini golf. Then he added, "We can cross out Number Ten. There was no one at dinner but all of us. And your backpack was here the whole time."

"So what do we have?"

Kevin followed the numbers with his index finger. "It could be Serena. Or Mr. Sidhu. Or someone on the beach or at mini golf. Or . . . your parents?" He looked up at me for approval.

I nodded. "Go on."

"Still . . . I bet it's either that guy in the restaurant or Marty."

"Okay, how do we figure out who it is?"

"We have to ask them all," Kevin said. "We don't have any choice."

"You said, 'we.' You still want to help?"

Kevin nodded.

"Even if it means something bad might happen to G-Mags?"

Kevin's eyes welled up. "I believe you'd do anything to save G-Mags, just like I would."

I looked away. "You understand that tomorrow morning you will have forgotten all of this?"

"It's hard to believe, but . . ."

"Can I ask you something?"

"Sure."

"What do you think I should say tomorrow morning to convince you I'm telling the truth?"

Kevin kicked a rock off the porch. "Tell me about

G-Mags again. After a while, just like today, I'll realize you'd never joke about something like that."

"Is that it? That'll make you want to help me?"

"Tell me about your mom being pregnant right away. I know how much you've always wanted a brother or sister. And tell me about how I'll never see Michael again."

I put the paints in my backpack. "Are you sure that'll be enough? I'll need you to believe that we already filmed the day and figured out who the suspects are."

Kevin thought for a minute. "I've got it! I'll tell you something that only Michael and I know, something we've kept a secret forever."

"What is it?"

Kevin leaned all the way across the table and whispered, "Once, when I was little, I took out one of Michael's baseballs and started throwing it in the air and catching it. The ball hit a glass clown that my mother loved, and I ran crying to Michael. He found some Krazy Glue and glued the clown's hat back on so I wouldn't get in trouble. Then the next day, he used his allowance to buy another clown. But he made me promise to never play ball in the house again—and to pay him back one day."

"Did you?"

Kevin nodded.

"So, if I tell you this secret, you'll believe everything else?"

"I think so."

"Okay. That's what I'll tell you."

CHAPTER 32

The next morning, I rewrote the names and places, adding the stars and color-coding. And as soon as I got to Annie's, I texted Kevin and ordered breakfast for both of us.

Once he arrived, I waited until he finished his egg and sausage bagel before reciting the story of the time loop, saving his secret for last.

He looked at me, wide-eyed, then put his face in his hands. Finally, he raised his head. "There's no way you'd know that secret if I hadn't told you."

"That's what you said yesterday." I slid the paper I'd worked on across the table. "These are the suspects."

"This doesn't look familiar at all," he said.

"We worked on it together."

"I know you wouldn't lie to me. But this is so weird." He studied the list. "So you said we've already ruled out Annie, right?" He glanced toward the counter where she was adjusting Joey's hairnet.

"It's definitely not Annie."

"Okay, then." He got up from the booth. "On to Serena."

Breathing a huge sigh of relief, I followed Kevin out the door. I still thought he was wrong about Serena being a suspect, but it was a good idea to ask her about the paints. She'd been an artist since she was my age, so she might recognize the box. And even if Kevin was right, and she had given me the paints, I was sure she'd done it to surprise me—not to ruin my life.

"So, let me get this straight," Kevin said. "How will it help to find out where the paints came from?"

"I need to find the instructions. There must be some explanation about how the magic works. If I can find that out, maybe I can reverse what's happening." As the blazing sun beat down on us, I wanted more than ever for summer to be over.

"Okay, I get it," Kevin said as we passed the funnel cake stand. "What's our strategy?"

The sweet smell of fried dough and sugar distracted me for a second. "I don't know. What do you think we should do?"

"Get right to the point. Pull out the paints and ask Serena if she gave them to you."

"Really? Isn't that kind of rude? Shouldn't we talk a little like we usually do and then ask if she's ever seen the paints before? You know, ease into it before accusing her."

Kevin looked at me with a serious expression. "We don't have time for that. Besides, there's a difference between asking and accusing. It's all in the tone."

After arriving at Serena's spot, we watched as she drew the last red polka dot on the little girl's bow. "Now can I have an ice-cream cone?" the girl asked.

As the mother and daughter left for the frozen custard stand, Serena turned to us and sighed. "Some people really don't appreciate art."

I nodded with sympathy, remembering how some

of my teachers would stand over me and frown when they saw me drawing in the margins of my notebook pages. But, like Kevin had said, there was no time for nice conversation. I took out the paints and shoved them in front of her.

Serena squinted up at me, startled.

"I'm sorry," I said, giving Kevin a sideways glance. "I didn't mean to be rude. I, uh, was wondering if you've ever seen these paints before."

She took the box and turned it over. "They look pretty old. Where did you get them?"

Was she faking innocence? "Someone gave them to me."

"Really? Seems like a weird gift." She shook the box. "How much do you want for them?"

"What? No. I don't want to sell them. I just want to know where they came from."

"Why don't you ask the person who gave them to you?"

"I, um, wanted to see if I could return the paints to get something else. And . . . I don't want to hurt the person's feelings." No matter how much I'd learned to lie all those weeks, it still felt so wrong.

Serena gave me a strange look. "I don't think you'll have much luck returning them. It seems like they might have come from a thrift shop or somewhere like that. They wouldn't be too interested in getting these paints back."

A thrift shop! Why didn't I think of that?

She opened the box and pulled out the tube of red paint. "Looks like someone's already used them."

As she twisted the cap off, I snatched the tube from her.

"We've got to get going now," Kevin said. "Do you know if there's a thrift shop around here?"

I shot him a look of gratitude. I couldn't let her use that paint. Who knew what might happen? And I sure didn't wish that magic on anyone.

Serena pointed down the boardwalk. "There's one about a mile that way and a couple of blocks west." She put her hand on the brim of her hat, right next to the grapes. "I bought this hat there."

"It's a great hat," I said as she handed me the paint box. Kevin and I thanked her for her help and moved on.

"I told you it wasn't Serena," I whispered, mentally crossing her off our list.

"So what do we do now?" Kevin asked. "Try the thrift store?"

"I don't think so. It'll throw our whole schedule off. Let's do what we normally do."

"You've got a point. We can go there later."

Next stop was Mr. Sidhu's store. As soon as we entered, I headed for the counter and plopped my backpack on it. Startled, Mr. Sidhu almost dropped his book.

"Sorry," I said. "I was wondering . . . does this backpack look familiar to you?"

"It is yours. Is it not?"

"Yes, but could you have . . . possibly placed something inside it by mistake?"

"No. I do not think so."

"Are you sure? Maybe someone bought something, and you put it in my backpack instead of theirs."

Mr. Sidhu put his hand to his chin. "I suppose it is possible. Did you find something in there that you did not buy?"

"Yes, yes!" At last, I was getting somewhere. My hand shook as I pulled the zipper open to reveal the yellow box.

Mr. Sidhu stared inside my backpack for a long

while. He seemed to be waiting, maybe for just the right words to tell me he was the one who gave me the paints. Maybe not even by accident.

Holding my breath, I waited for him to confess.

After a while, he began, "I am sorry but . . ."

I nearly shouted the words: "But what? What are you sorry about?"

"I do not see the book you received by mistake?"

I pulled out the paints. "It's not a book. It's this!"

He stared at the box, his bushy eyebrows coming together as one.

"Do you recognize these?" I asked, filled with anticipation.

He looked from the paints to me and shook his head.

Kevin grabbed the box from my hand and turned toward the other customers. "Has anyone ever seen paints like this before?" he shouted.

Some people glanced at him and shook their heads. Most went about their business.

Defeated, I grabbed the paints and shoved them into my backpack. We apologized to Mr. Sidhu for bothering him and left the store.

"Well," Kevin said. "That was a bust."

"I guess I didn't really think it was him."

"Yeah," Kevin said. "He's a nice guy, but he's not in the business of giving away stuff."

"So, what do we do now?"

Kevin pointed straight ahead. "On to the beach!"

Once we were in the water, Kevin and I kept our eyes on our backpacks. After observing the couple next to our beach towels for a while, I whispered to Kevin, "That couple hasn't been watching our stuff at all."

"But do you really think someone on the beach gave you the paints?"

I shrugged and kept a lookout for anyone suspicious-looking. After a while I noticed something I hadn't seen those other days. The girl with the long, dark hair, the one I saw every time I was getting the water for the stegosaurus spikes, was walking right by our stuff. She waved to her friend and then suddenly dropped to the sand. Had she lost something? I couldn't see what she was doing. I jumped up and down in the water to get a better look, but there were too many people in the way. By the time I could see her again, she'd already met her friend, and they were settling their stuff in the sand.

Could she have given me the paints? I pointed her out to Kevin.

"If she already gave you the paints, why would she be by our backpacks now?"

"Returning to the scene of the crime?"

"Why would she do that?"

"I don't know, but I've heard people do that sometimes. I've got to find out if she's the one. Keep your eye out for anyone else who goes near our stuff."

Once I got to my backpack, I took out the yellow box and trudged over to the two girls, who were lying in the sun with their eyes closed. My feet burned as I stood next to their blanket. "Um, excuse me," I said.

The dark-haired girl opened her eyes.

"I . . . I don't know your name, but I'm Haleigh, and . . . I found these paints on the beach, and I was wondering if they were yours."

The girl sat up on her elbows and squinted up at me. "It's Megan." She took the box. "Where did you find them?"

I pointed to where my stuff was. "Over there."

She shook her head and turned toward her friend. "Hey, Kate, have you ever seen these on the beach?"

Kate looked at them and lay back down.

"You sure they don't belong to you?" I asked.

Megan shook her head, and then all of a sudden her eyes widened. "You're the girl I've seen sketching on the boardwalk sometimes."

My feet were on fire now. She was probably thinking, *nerd alert*.

"You're good," she said. "I wish I could draw like that."

I almost fell down in shock. "Really?"

Just as she started to answer me, Kate sat up. "Oh yeah," she said. "You're the one who's always hanging out with that cute boy. Is he your boyfriend?"

"Uh, no," I said. "We're just friends." I didn't add that we might get to be more than friends if the time loop ended. But that wasn't something I was ready to talk about—especially to a couple of girls I didn't know.

Megan beamed. "We should all hang out. Like tomorrow, maybe?"

"We're going home tomorrow," I said.

Megan frowned. "Well, maybe next summer." She handed me the yellow box. "You should keep those paints. They look used. Whoever lost them probably doesn't care."

"You're right," I said. "Sorry to bother to you."

As I slogged through the sand back to my towel, I thought about how jealous I'd been of Megan. When, all along, she and her friend had been kind of jealous of me, too.

I wondered how many times I'd been wrong about other people's feelings. How many times I'd imagined they felt one way, but it was really the opposite. Like with Kevin. I'd almost convinced myself that our friendship would fizzle out, just like the others had. But maybe it was me that hadn't tried hard enough all those times.

Right then, I promised myself if I ever got out of the time loop, I'd send Abbey another text.

And I'd stop jumping to conclusions about people's feelings. At least I'd try to.

CHAPTER 33

"Okay," Kevin said as we stepped inside G-Mags's cottage. "We've ruled out Serena, Mr. Sidhu, and anyone on the beach. But we still have plenty of suspects in Atlantic City."

"I really hope we find what we're looking for there."

"What's this?" G-Mags came out of the kitchen with a concerned look. "Did you lose something?"

Kevin shook his head. "We were just trying to figure out who gave Haleigh a box of pai—"

"Painful moments!" I yelled, shooting Kevin a look of warning. "I thought I'd lost my backpack for a minute, and I had some really painful moments thinking I'd lost it."

"That's a relief," G-Mags said. "Come now, there's nothing that fresh cannolis can't fix. Let's get started." She headed back into the kitchen.

I turned to Kevin and whispered, "We can't tell her about the paints. If we do, then we'd have to tell her everything."

"Oh, sorry. But are you sure we can't prevent her from having a stroke? I know you promised you tried really hard. But are you positive?"

"Yes. We both tried."

Kevin rubbed the back of his neck. "I wish I could remember."

I kept expecting Kevin to know what I knew. But I had to remind myself he'd known about the time loop for only a few hours. "Trust me, the only thing we can do to prevent G-Mags from having a stroke every night is to find out where the paints came from."

"I believe you. I guess if we can't prevent it, there's no reason to tell her what will happen tonight."

"Right."

"And if the time loop stops, she could be fine

tomorrow, once the doctors take care of her." His face looked hopeful.

"That's right," I said. But I knew we couldn't be sure.

As I helped G-Mags with the cannolis, the smell of vanilla, sweet and pungent at the same time, was almost overwhelming. I gripped the wooden spoon with both hands as I stirred.

Once we were done, Kevin and I decided to head to the thrift store before our trip to Atlantic City.

"What exactly are we looking for at this place?" Kevin said. "Do you think they have more paints like yours?"

"I don't know, but it's worth a try. Maybe if they do, I can find out if the instructions in another box will tell me how to reverse the magic."

"Good plan," Kevin said. He was quiet for a while, until we were way past where we usually walked. He gestured toward the Ferris wheel on the pier. "We never got around to riding it."

"I feel like I've been riding it all summer."

"What do you mean?"

"You know, going round and round, but not getting anywhere."

"I didn't think about how it felt for you," Kevin said over all the noise from the kids and the rides. "Has it been awful?"

The music from the Ferris wheel got softer as we headed west. "It was great in the beginning. I loved all the things we did that last day. But then it got kind of boring."

We stopped to cross the street, and Kevin looked at me. "How many times have you relived today?"

The WALK sign appeared. "I lost count. Maybe fifty or sixty."

"Wow. That's a lot of ragout and cannolis."

"And don't forget the Italian ice, the saltwater taffy, and the taco place I could never talk you out of."

Kevin smiled, but then gave me a puzzled look. "How come we didn't get fat?"

"I don't know. That's not how it works. But I'll tell you one thing: when I get back home, I might join my mom on her health food kick."

We were both quiet until we got to the thrift shop. The two of us strolled past racks and racks of shirts, pants, sweaters, coats, and even costumes in all sizes and styles. Kevin stopped to pull out a Darth Vader suit.

"Whoa, this is vintage *Star Wars*. I've seen stuff like this on eBay for like fifty dollars." He looked at the price. "Three ninety-nine! Obi-Wan Kenobi! That's a steal!"

I took the hanger from Kevin and examined the costume. "Why would someone give this away if they could sell it for fifty dollars?"

"Obviously, they had no idea they were in possession of one of the greatest costumes of all time." He tucked the outfit under his arm. "Some people just don't know the value of things."

Even though he wasn't talking about me, his words stung. I had no idea how great my life had been before the time loop. I gestured to the costume under Kevin's arm. "Aren't you going to put it back?"

"Are you kidding? I have to buy this."

"You know, you probably won't get to keep it. Even if we stop the time loop, your August twenty-sixth might not be this one. It might be the day I did the painting."

"It's okay. Even if I have it for only a little while, it'll be really cool."

I followed him toward the back of the store. About twenty boxes full of books, record albums, and old toys sat in rows against a wall. We went through all of them, rummaging around hundreds of Happy Meal figures, bags full of broken crayons and chalk, and stacks of half-used workbooks. I held a torn *Sleeping Beauty* coloring book in the air. "Why would anyone think people want this junk?"

Kevin held up a New Jersey Devils bobblehead with a spring that was already sprung. "Like my mom always says, 'One man's rubbish is another man's riches.'" He put the bobblehead aside and dug deep into the box. Then he looked up with a gleam in his eyes. "And what do we have here?" He yanked out a banged up yellow carton that read: OIL PAINTS.

I snatched it from his hands.

"Slow down," Kevin said. "Let's investigate before we get too excited."

I shoved the box toward him. "You open it. I'm too nervous."

He released the flap and stuck his hand inside. He pulled out a tube of black paint and a small, folded piece of paper.

I took the box back and shook it. There were more paints inside. I turned it over in my sweaty palms and held my breath to see if it read: *Paint your heart's desire.*

It didn't. Still hopeful, I grabbed the folded page from Kevin.

"What does it say?" he asked. "Anything about magic?"

My fingers tingled as I read.

But when I got to the end, I crumpled the paper and threw it on the floor.

Kevin picked it up as I collapsed onto a nearby chair with a torn seat cushion. "What's wrong? What is it?"

"They're just directions on how to use oil paints—stuff I already know." I kicked one of the boxes. "I'll never find out how these dumb paints work!"

"I'm sorry," Kevin said. "It was a long shot, anyway." He looked at the mess of junk. "We better get back home so we can go to Atlantic City."

He paid for his Darth Vader costume, and we headed out the door. "I wish I could show this to Michael. He'd think it was so cool."

"You know," I said. "I really hope I get to meet Michael someday."

"Me too," Kevin said, picking up his pace. "We definitely need to find those directions."

CHAPTER 34

My heart pounded as I waited for the man in the black suit with the briefcase to take his seat behind me. There were only a few suspects left.

Kevin picked up the straw and blew the paper my way. I deliberately missed and let it fall to the floor.

We looked at the menus and started our usual conversation. Once we started talking about art and my sketches, the man began eavesdropping. I could tell because of the look on Kevin's face. I'd observed pretty much every expression he could possibly have during the time loop. And I knew what they all meant.

When two parallel lines appeared between his eyebrows, he was sad.

When the dimple in his left cheek deepened, he was happy.

And when his eyebrows raised just enough to meet the hair that was always falling forward, I knew something weird had happened.

As Kevin and I talked more about my sketches and Michael's job as a graphic artist, I realized the man always started listening to our conversation when we began talking about drawing and illustrating. He was obviously interested in art. Maybe the paints were his at one time, and he wanted to pass them along to someone he knew would appreciate them. Maybe even welcome their magic.

Why hadn't I figured that out sooner? It had to be him!

When the man leaned down to pick up the paper, I snuck a look to the floor to see if he seemed suspicious. I held my breath as I watched to see if he went near my backpack.

No. But I knew that didn't mean anything. He would have already given me the paints.

He could still be our guy.

I reached down to get a pencil from my backpack and then scribbled on a napkin for Kevin: *I think he's the one. Let's eat fast so we can tail him when he leaves.*

Kevin took the pencil from me and wrote: *Tail him? I think you've been watching too many detective shows.*

I wrote back: *Ha ha. Just eat fast!*

The second after I took my last crunch of taco, the man's chair scraped behind me.

Kevin and I threw enough money to cover the bill and tip onto the table and followed him out the door.

"He could be dangerous," Kevin whispered. "Let's get to him before he goes down a dark hallway or someplace where there's no one to hear us scream."

"Scream?" My mouth went dry. Still, I had to know. I raced toward the man, who was taller than he'd looked when he was sitting in the restaurant, and tapped his back.

He twirled and gave me a look of surprise. "You're the girl who was sitting behind me—the artist," he said with a British accent.

I straightened up and answered, "Yes. Why were you listening to us?"

Kevin came up beside me. "Yeah," he said. "What's the deal?"

The man gave a puzzled look. "Did we make a deal? I'm not aware."

"Don't act dumb," Kevin said. "You were eavesdropping on our conversation the whole time."

"Oh dear. Was it that obvious? Did I seem a bit dodgy?"

"Dodgy?" Kevin said.

"Ah, how do you say it in the States . . . sketchy? I didn't mean to make you uncomfortable. But as an art dealer, I'm always interested when I see a young person who wants to become an artist. There are so few people left these days who care about art and painting."

"Painting?" I said.

"Yes. You know, all anyone is interested in today is the so-called art they make on their computers—or photographs they take with their cell phones." He shook his head. "Awful stuff. It's tragic, really."

As he spoke, I unzipped my backpack and pulled out the yellow box. "Then maybe you could tell me if you've seen paints like these before." My hands shook as I held the box out to him.

The man examined it without saying anything.

I watched his reaction, adding, "I found them back in the restaurant. I thought they might be yours."

He gave a half smile. He was the one! I knew it!

I was all ready with my next question when he exclaimed, "How sweet of you! Not many people would have chased after me to return them."

My knees shook with anticipation. "Please, please tell me about their magic."

The man's forehead wrinkled. "Magic?"

"Yes, you must know about it if they belong to you."

"Oh. No. You misunderstood me. They're not *my* paints. I was just impressed that you took the time to look for the owner."

My arms dropped to my sides as I let out a huge sigh of disappointment.

"So sorry I couldn't help you now," the man said, taking his wallet from his pocket. He pulled out a card. "But one day when you're a great artist, give me a call, and I'll help you sell your paintings."

I took the card and read: *Alexander McElwain, Art Dealer.* When I looked up, he had a big smile on his face. "Good luck to you," he said before walking away.

I turned to Kevin. "He wasn't that creepy after all, was he?"

Kevin shook his head. "I guess not."

I shoved the paints back into my bag. "What now?"

Kevin pointed to Marty's Magic Shop and raised his eyebrows. "It's showtime!"

CHAPTER 35

Marty pulled the scarf from my backpack, and I felt my face flush like it did the first day I was there. This time it was more nerves than embarrassment. I had to get Marty away from the crowd so he'd admit he put the yellow box in my backpack.

We were running out of suspects, and I was starting to think Kevin had been right about Marty. After all the "oohs" and "aahs," he gave his usual sales pitch. As soon as he finished, I tapped him on the shoulder. There was a strange gleam in his eyes when he turned to me and asked, "You interested in buying something?"

"Uh, no," I said, trying to steady my voice. "I was wondering if you sell magic paints?"

The gleam disappeared as Marty shook his head and turned to talk to someone else.

At that moment, Kevin chimed in, "I might be interested in buying that scarf trick. Can you show it to me?"

I gave him a grateful look as we followed Marty to the counter. Kevin pretended to be interested in all the tricks for sale, while I unzipped my bag. As soon as there was a pause in the conversation, I pulled out the box. "I was wondering if you have a trick where I could hide something this big up my sleeve."

"That would be some trick," Marty said. His eyes narrowed. "Hey, weren't you the girl just asking me about magic paints?"

"Yes . . ." Was he about to confess?

He pointed to the yellow box. "Are those yours?"

I nodded, bursting inside with the anticipation of finally figuring out the mystery. I couldn't hold it in any longer. "It was you!" I shouted. "It was you!"

"Hey, listen, kid." His voice sounded gruff. "I didn't do anything." He looked around as he twirled the end of his mustache. "Put that old box away before customers think I'm selling some kind of used tricks in here."

"You mean you didn't put this in my backpack when you took the scarf out?"

"Are you kidding? If I could do a trick like that, I wouldn't be working in a hotel magic shop. I'd be doing shows in Vegas."

Disappointment flooded through me. "Thanks, anyway," I mumbled.

"We still have another shot," Kevin said as we headed toward the boardwalk. "Maybe it was someone at mini golf. Or . . . I don't know, but we can't give up."

I forced myself to smile. "No, we can't."

But I was beginning to lose hope.

"Wow," Kevin said, "a hole in one. I guess you've gotten pretty good with all the practice."

"This and my artwork. That part's been good."

As Kevin took his shot, I noticed that the three boys behind us, who looked about my age, were all carrying backpacks. The two girls had only small purses on their shoulders. Any one of those boys could have slipped the paints inside my bag when I ran to help Kevin. But how could I find out which one? I couldn't just go up to them and ask, "Hey, did you give me magic paints?"

With my mind deep in thought, it took me eight tries on the next hole. Kevin hit the ball in with his usual two shots. Watching him gave me an idea. I whispered my plan in his ear.

On the next hole, I took thirteen tries to get the ball in.

Kevin groaned loudly. "C'mon. We'll never finish the course at this rate." He pretended to storm off to the next hole.

While everyone was looking at him, I took out the paints and placed them on the ground at the Peter Pan hole. I moved on, surveying the group of kids as they approached the wooden pirate ship. I figured once they found the yellow box, I'd be able to tell by their reactions if one of them was the culprit.

As they neared the hole, they were having such a good time that no one noticed the box.

I waited and waited. Nothing.

After a few minutes, I walked back to where the

kids were laughing and making fun of each other. They ignored me as I passed them and picked up the paints. "Whew, that was close!" I said it like I was an actor in a play, and the back row needed to hear me. All five kids turned. I waved the box in the air. "These must have fallen out of my backpack." I knew they thought I was totally crazy, but that was my last chance to solve the mystery. "Have any of you seen these types of paints before?" I asked. "They didn't come with directions."

One of the guys, who wore a Yankees cap, looked closer at the box. "They're oil paints," he said, grinning. "Why do you need directions? Don't you just, duh, paint with them?"

The rest of the kids laughed.

It *was* kind of a dumb question. Before the time loop, I would have been embarrassed, but I had more important issues to deal with. "Are you sure you've never seen paints like these?"

One of the girls, the one who hadn't giggled as much, took a closer look. "These seem really old. They're probably from before we were even born. Where did you get them?"

"Someone gave them to me," I answered.

"You should give them back!" the boy with the cap bellowed.

Then all five kids burst into laughter again.

I laughed along with them, as if the guy actually said something funny.

But, deep down, all I felt was despair. Maybe whoever had given me the paints didn't even remember. Maybe that person's memory was wiped clean every morning like everyone else's.

I was beginning to think I was stuck with those paints.

Just like I was stuck in summer.

CHAPTER 36

Usually Kevin and I were watching the end of *The Day the Earth Stood Still* before dinner, but that evening I couldn't bear to watch it one more time. Kevin and I had totally run out of suspects. And even though we'd agreed to keep looking, I'd almost given up hope.

I sat on a kitchen chair next to the stove and stared down at the fossil in my hand, the one I'd found every morning since the time loop had started.

"You look sad," G-Mags said. "Is there something upsetting you?"

Of course, I couldn't tell her what was wrong. So, I held out the piece of rock and asked if she'd like to see it. "It has a fish skeleton on it."

G-Mags turned the rock over in her palm. "Isn't it lovely the way nature provides us this way of remembering what came before us?"

"What do you mean?"

"Fossils are nature's way of revealing our history. An imprint of a tiny fish like this one on your rock is a way of telling us that there was life before us, and it will continue long after we're gone. It's as if the fish is crying out, *Remember me.*" She pressed the rock back into my palm. "Nature is quite the artist, isn't she?"

"I never thought of it that way," I said, sliding the rock into my pocket. I pictured my own artwork and how everything I added to my sketchbook each day was always gone the next morning. When I flipped open my pad, there was no record of my having sketched anything at all. It was as if I'd been drawing with disappearing ink.

And day after day, just like my sketches, history was being erased too.

As Kevin joined us and repeated the words *Klaatu*

barada nikto, sadness washed over me. In the movie, the phrase could bring someone back to life. But those words seemed hollow and empty to me.

I blinked back tears.

"What's wrong, dear?" G-Mags said. "Are you sure there isn't something you'd like to talk about?"

I looked up at her concerned face. Maybe I could tell her *one* of my secrets.

I leaned in close and whispered, "Can I tell you something?"

"Of course, dear."

"It's a secret."

G-Mags pretended to zip her lips with her fingers.

"My mom is having a baby."

G-Mags clapped her hands and whispered, "What a lovely surprise." But her eyes didn't seem like she was surprised at all.

After a few seconds she said, "Speaking of secrets, that reminds me about something I wanted to give you before everyone left. I'll be right back."

I gazed around the kitchen and living room. Even after all those nights, I loved looking at the Damico family treasures. My eyes fell on the painting of Kevin, and it reminded me that I might never get to meet Michael—or my own brother or sister.

My heart ached at the thought. I got up to examine the painting further. I was studying Michael's signature at the bottom of the painting, noticing his distinctive loop on the *M*, when something hit me. The year under the signature: it couldn't have been right.

I whipped around to face G-Mags as she returned to the living room. "Did Michael make a mistake on the date when he painted this?"

"I don't think so."

"But it's impossible. This painting of Kevin was done the year before he was born."

G-Mags broke out into a huge smile. "That was what made it so special. Michael was always asking for a little brother to play with. For years that was all he talked about. Then one day when he was visiting, he was bored and restless. I pulled out a set of paints I'd found in a closet when I moved into this house. I gave them to him, and he painted this picture of a little boy."

Was she saying what I thought she was saying? I resisted the urge to jump up and down and scream.

"At the time, we just thought it was a nice painting.

But several years later, when Kevin was about three years old, we all noticed the resemblance between him and the portrait. We couldn't believe what a coincidence it was."

Was it a coincidence? Had Michael painted his heart's desire to have a little brother? My own heart raced as I took a deep breath and asked, "And, where are these paints now?"

"That's the strange thing," G-Mags said. "I was just looking for the box—I wanted to surprise you, but I can't find it anywhere." She walked over to the end table where she kept her teacup and Bible.

I froze in my spot. My heart pounded so hard it felt like it was trying to break free of my chest.

"I was sure the box was still in the closet," G-Mags said. "I tried to get Michael to take the paints with him years ago. But he said he had other paints at home, and he left them here."

I was still too shocked to move. All those nights that G-Mags had been talking about giving me something in the morning, she'd been talking about the paints. It was all so clear now: she must have snuck the box in my backpack to surprise me on that first August twenty-sixth. But of course, the next day she wouldn't have remembered she'd done it.

Slowly, I made my way to the couch and collapsed into the soft cushions. I knew the next decision I made could alter the course of all of our lives. Did I dare ask G-Mags if she knew about the magic?

I had to. But first I needed to know something else.

I sat up straight. "What if I told you that you already gave me those paints—and they were magic?"

G-Mags gave a little laugh. "I would say you must have stayed out in the sun too long today."

"Well, let's say, just for fun, they had the power to stop time. Would you want that?"

Without hesitation, G-Mags responded, "Heavens no!"

"You wouldn't want to live forever?"

"Of course not, dear. It wouldn't be right. It's not the way the world works, now, is it?"

"But what if it *were* the way the world works? Would you want to live forever?"

"I can't imagine a world where I would have the choice. But if I did, I'm afraid I'd choose not to."

"Why? Why wouldn't you want to live forever?"

She reached toward the side table and picked up her Bible. Flipping to a page with a folded corner, she said, "Here's your answer—it's my favorite passage from the Old Testament."

I took the Bible from her and silently read:

To every thing there is a season, and a time to every purpose under the heaven:

A time to be born, and a time to die; a time to plant, and a time to pluck up that which is planted

I stopped there because my eyes stung and the words had gotten blurry. "But what if there didn't have to be a time to die?" I said. "What if you could just stay the same forever—what if we could all stay the same forever, here on the shore?"

G-Mags sat down next to me. "As much as I love you all, I wouldn't want everything to stay the same. It wouldn't be fair, now, would it? You and Kevin should have a chance to grow up and maybe someday have children of your own. That's the way it's supposed to be."

"But what if you weren't there to see Kevin grow up? Would that make you sad?"

G-Mags sighed. "Of course I'd be sad, but that's the way life goes. We die and make room for another generation. It's painful, but that's why we have memory. To keep people alive in our hearts." She pressed her hand to her chest. "But why all these questions from a young girl like you? You shouldn't be thinking about these things. You should be thinking about the beach and school and parties."

I put the Bible down on the couch. "I guess I just don't want summer to end."

G-Mags gave me a long hug. "I don't blame you, dear. It's been a wonderful time, hasn't it? But consider how awful it would be if you never again got to see a raindrop or a snowflake or the leaves of a sugar maple turn colors and fall to the ground?"

"I never thought of that."

She grabbed a piece of paper from her housecoat pocket. "I'm sorry I couldn't surprise you with Michael's paints. But maybe these directions will help you with your artwork, anyway. They must have fallen out of the box, and I didn't see them on the closet floor."

Suddenly, I couldn't breathe. I steadied my hand as I reached out to take the paper from her. For something containing so much power, it felt weightless in my hand.

Flap by flap, I unfolded the directions and read. When I reached the bottom of the page, I nearly fainted.

I pulled my phone from my backpack on the floor and doubled over, groaning with exaggeration.

Startled, G-Mags put her arm around me.

Kevin came running from the kitchen. "What happened?" he asked. "What's wrong?"

I leaned back on the cushion. "I'm okay. It was just a stomach cramp. Maybe some water would help." As G-Mags scurried away, I whispered to Kevin, "I figured it out. I've got to get home fast to change the painting."

His eyes widened. "How? How do you know?"

I showed him the directions. "Are you sure you want me to do it? With all your heart, are you sure you want me to make time move forward? No matter what happens?"

He thought for almost a full minute. "Yes," he said. "It's the right thing to do."

I punched the buttons on the phone and asked my dad to come and get me.

CHAPTER 37

I'd touched the painting that morning—and a smudge of blue had come off on my finger. The directions said a wish could be reversed as long as the paint hadn't dried. I hoped there was still time.

The second I walked in the house, I raced toward my desk. But the painting wasn't there. I dashed to the closet. After shuffling things around, I still couldn't find it. Had I put it somewhere else? I looked on my dresser, behind the bedroom door, even under my bed. But it was nowhere.

I couldn't think straight. "Mom, Mom!"

At first there was no answer. I screamed louder and both my parents came running. "What's wrong? You said you felt better once you came home."

"I'm fine. I'm fine."

Mom put her cheek against my forehead.

I pulled away. "Stop! I need to talk to you. Did either of you see a painting in my room?"

"Haleigh!" Mom said. "You have to calm down. I think you have a fever. Let me see if I have anything for it." She left the room.

"No!" I called after her. "I just need the painting. Where is it?"

Dad put his arm around me. "Why don't you lie down? You'll feel better."

"No, I won't. Don't you see? I'm running out of time."

Mom rushed into the room with a wet cloth in her hands. "Is she okay?"

"I don't know," Dad said. "The fever might be making her delirious. She keeps saying something about running out of time."

Mom pressed the cold compress against my forehead. "Now, close your eyes," she said, softly. "Calm down."

I realized my parents weren't going to leave my room until they were convinced I was okay. I took a few deep breaths and steadied myself.

"That's much better," Dad said. "Now, what's this about a painting?"

"Oh," Mom said. "I know what she's talking about. I found a painting in here this morning. It was still wet, so I put it on the porch to dry." She looked at me. "I was just about to bring it in here when you called us."

I bolted upright, grabbed Mom's hand, and put it against my forehead. Her eyes opened wide as she looked at Dad. "She seems to be fine now."

"I told you I'm okay." I jumped up from the bed. "I can start packing now."

I waited until their footsteps faded and then flew to the porch to retrieve the painting.

I dabbed my finger against the bottom, where I'd made thick clumps to resemble sand.

The paint was still wet. Yes!

Once I was in my room, I opened the instruction

booklet and went straight to the *Paint Your Heart's Desire* heading. The directions explained that if you wanted your deepest desire to come true, you had to paint with that longing in your heart at the time.

I thought back to when I first saw the yellow box in my backpack. All I wanted then was for summer to never end. I hadn't even needed to wish on the painting—that desire had been in my heart all along.

I continued to read:

> *Once you have finished painting your heart's desire, put your canvas aside for the oil to dry. If by chance you change your mind, as long as the paint has not dried, you may undo your desire by adding to the canvas or by painting over what is already there. Make sure, however, that you know what's truly in your heart. You will have only one chance to undo your original wish.*

My hands shook as I removed the paints from the box. I couldn't make a mistake this time. I had to be sure of what I wanted to do, sure of what was in my heart.

Something terrible could happen if the next day wasn't August twenty-sixth anymore. But, after all those weeks, I truly understood what G-Mags meant when she bowed her head and whispered, "May she rest in peace."

I needed to let G-Mags rest in peace if it was her time. I couldn't let her keep having a stroke every night.

And there were lots of other reasons to want time to move forward. I made a mental list: Kevin would be able to put all his footage together to make that sci-fi movie he was always working on. And, he'd get to see Michael again.

The seeds Mom had gotten from G-Mags would grow into herbs. Mom would get to finish her book about van Gogh. And, according to the website I'd looked at, once she was past a certain point in her pregnancy, her indigestion could get better.

Dad could continue his research on time and space.

Mr. Damico could finally get some new trivia.

I'd get to take art classes and keep my drawings. And maybe even see Abbey again.

But, most important, I'd be getting a new brother or sister.

I propped up the canvas and squeezed a few blobs of black and white paint on the palette. I added the linseed oil, and the smell took me back to the night I'd first used the paints.

My eyes burned and my heart felt like it was rising into my throat as I whispered over and over: "I wish for time to move forward. I wish for time to move forward. I wish . . ."

I opened my eyes and kept whispering as I threw globs of gray on the upper portion of the canvas. The weather report for the next day had called for rain, so I swirled the paint in circles, to make clouds like the ones in van Gogh's *The Starry Night*. I didn't stop whispering until the clouds were finished, and there was no turning back.

I sighed as I put the painting on my desk and grabbed my suitcase from the closet. It was a bittersweet feeling, knowing that might be the last time I'd be packing. As I pressed each piece of clothing into the suitcase, I thought about how it had been a whole day of lasts.

My last ragout dinner.

My last day with Kevin on the beach.

My last time to hear Mateo's joke about saving time. Actually, that one wasn't so bad.

After tucking a couple of my fossils between some T-shirts, I closed the suitcase.

Then I crawled into bed and waited for the doorbell to ring.

CHAPTER 38

Seeing Kevin's face as he walked through the door made me feel even worse than I had that first night. I told myself I didn't know what would happen in the morning. G-Mags might be perfectly fine. But the look on everyone's faces made me realize that was wishful thinking.

As I pulled down the sheets on the couch, there was little I could say to offer encouragement to Kevin. All I could tell him was, "I'm so sorry," over and over.

He didn't look at me for a long while. But once he tugged the blanket under his chin he glanced my way and said, "It's okay. You didn't cause the stroke."

"I know but . . ." I couldn't look into his eyes.

"Did you do it?" he asked. "Did you fix the painting to reverse the magic?"

"Yes," I whispered. Now that he'd seen for himself what happened with G-Mags, could he have changed his mind? "Are you sure it's what you want?"

He hesitated, looking up at the ceiling.

"I saved some paint. The clouds I made are still wet. Maybe there's time to paint over them."

He thought for what seemed like a long, long time, but was probably only minutes. Then he looked at me with the saddest eyes I'd ever seen. "We're doing the right thing, aren't we? It's what she would want. Right?"

I looked away because I couldn't stand to see him so sad. "I think so."

After getting up the courage to say good night, I lay in bed, staring at the ceiling. My mind raced as I pictured what might happen the next day, and the next, and the next.

It was no use trying to sleep.

I got up and opened my sketchbook. As I took out my box of colored pencils, I realized that whatever I drew would be there in the morning. That was one good thing.

I remembered what G-Mags had said about fossils being like art, and began sketching a picture of my fossil with the fish skeleton. Beneath the picture, I wrote: *Nature's Memory.*

Underneath that, I drew a sugar maple tree with its leaves of vibrant reds, oranges, and yellows as they fell to the ground. Beside that, I drew a snowflake. And below both of them, I wrote: *A Time for Every Season.*

At the bottom of the page, I drew a full moon, shining against a dark sky. Under that, I wrote: *Full Moon Soon.*

Finally, exhaustion swept over me. I set my clock for seven and settled into bed. I gazed out the window at the moon, the same crescent moon I'd stared at night after night.

No longer a closed parenthesis, it seemed more like a giant comma, a pause in the middle of a sentence, ready for the rest to be written

CHAPTER 39

As soon as the alarm sounded, I squeezed my eyelids together even tighter. Holding my breath, I turned toward the desk.

With a mixture of emotions, I cracked an eye open to see if the gray clouds were still painted on the canvas.

They were.

It worked! The time loop had to be over. But I couldn't be totally sure until I saw the calendar. The night before, I'd ripped off the page that read *August 26* and thrown it in the garbage.

I raced to the kitchen. My pulse pounded as I

turned the corner, stopped, and read: *August 27.*

I let out a huge breath. Underneath the date was the new animal fact: *According to scientists, cows have best friends and become stressed if they are separated.*

I looked over at Kevin on the couch. Someday I'd have to tell him that one.

But right then, I had something more important to do.

I tiptoed back into my room and got out the yellow box. I needed to get rid of the paints. Even though they hadn't worked when I'd used them on paper, I couldn't be sure. What if someone evil found them?

I knew the paints would be toxic to the environment if I threw them away or squeezed them down the drain.

There was only one thing left to do.

I ripped out three pages from my sketchpad and scattered them all over the floor. Silence surrounded me as I took the blue paint and held it high above the first large sheet of paper. I squeezed the tube from the bottom, and a drop of paint was released. For a second it seemed to hang in midair above the floor, a small blue blob suspended in time.

My breath caught, and I wondered if this was really

what I wanted. Should I stop now? I asked myself. Should I save the paints in case they might work on another canvas? What if the future was even worse than I imagined?

I squeezed the sides of the tube so the remaining paint slithered back inside, like a snake going backward.

Still, a single blue drop splattered like a raindrop on the paper. I had to continue.

I squeezed out another drop of blue. Then another.

I did the same with the next two sheets of paper, rolling the paint tube from the bottom to make sure it was totally empty.

I did it all again with each tube: red, yellow, orange, green, purple, black, white, and brown.

Soon, colored dots decorated each page.

The sharp smell of paint enveloped me as I knelt before the first sheet with brush in hand. My eyes prickled.

There was no turning back. Once I swirled the paint across those pages, there definitely would be no more chances to change the future or stop something bad from happening.

After a few deep breaths, I swept the brush across the first page. I continued making broad brushstrokes on each sheet, mixing the colors together in energetic swirls like the yin and yang symbol in the middle of van Gogh's *The Starry Night*.

When the paintings were finished, I stood and examined them. Each one was different, with its own blend of hues, its own mood. I checked the paint tubes again, making sure I'd squeezed out every drop.

The smell flooded my mind with memories of Kevin and G-Mags and the day I found the paints. It seemed both long ago and just like the day before.

Finally, I threw the brush into the yellow box with the flattened tubes of paint and took it all to the garbage can in the backyard.

When I returned, Kevin was still sleeping on the couch. I figured he probably wouldn't remember anything about the paints or the time loop when he woke up. His last day of summer would likely be the one that happened so many weeks before. The only thing on his mind this morning would be G-Mags. And no matter what, we wouldn't be eating breakfast together at Annie's.

I tiptoed into the kitchen and stared through blurry eyes at the lone apple in the fruit bowl on the table, the one Mom had thrown my way every day for weeks. I'd always thrown it back to her. But that morning, I clutched the apple in my hand and took a huge bite. The tartness tingled my jaw as the juice seeped from the corner of my mouth, down to my chin. I wiped it with the back of my hand.

And waited for the future to happen.

CHAPTER 40

Less than fifteen minutes later, the doorbell rang, and I rushed to answer it. I found Kevin's mother, alone on the porch. After a few seconds my parents arrived, and Kevin ran into his mother's arms.

No one said anything. But we all understood.

We exchanged sad hugs before Kevin left with his mom so they could "make arrangements." I'd always associated that phrase with something else: making a flower arrangement or making an arrangement to meet someone. But that day, I learned it had another meaning. A much sadder one.

Once we were alone, Mom, Dad, and I looked at each other, not sure what to do next. We were almost packed and ready to leave for home, but none of us seemed to want to move. I could tell Mom and Dad didn't want to believe what happened to G-Mags. They wanted to hang on to summer as much as I had all those weeks ago.

As we sat around the kitchen table, I got an idea. I leaped off my chair and headed to the refrigerator. Would the cannoli from G-Mags be in there? Would it still be fresh?

Yes! I grabbed it from the shelf and poked the shell. It was still crispy. I pulled out a dish and a knife, to cut the cannoli in three pieces. "This is the last one," I said, setting the plate before Mom and Dad. "Let's share it."

As I lifted the cannoli to my mouth, Mom stopped me. "Wait," she said. "Before we eat, let's remember G-Mags by sharing our favorite story about her."

I put the cannoli down to think of something. Before I could, Dad piped up, "I've got one."

Mom and I turned and listened.

"One evening when I came to pick you up, G-Mags had me sit at the table, and she put two of her delicious meatballs and some sauce in a dish for me."

I smiled, remembering how she loved to feed everyone. "That's a great memory."

"That's not all of it," Dad said. "Along with the food, she told me this wonderful story about Kevin's father when he was your age. Apparently, he tried to surprise G-Mags and her husband by raking the leaves in the backyard and then burning them."

"Burning them? Isn't that illegal?" I asked.

"Back then," Dad continued, "people didn't realize it was bad for the environment. And Mr. Damico also didn't realize what he was doing was dangerous. The flames spread to the neighbor's fence, and before he could put the fire out by throwing dirt on it, a portion of the fence was ruined."

It was hard to imagine Mr. Damico, with all his trivia and facts, being so careless. "So, then what happened?"

"When G-Mags found out, she made Mr. Damico go over and confess to the neighbors what he'd done."

"He must have been so scared."

"Yes. He begged G-Mags to tell them instead, but she told him he had to do it himself. However, she made a big pot of spaghetti and meatballs for him to bring over when he apologized." Dad smiled and got a twinkle in his eye. "What Mr. Damico didn't know at the time was that before he went over there, G-Mags had called the neighbors to tell them what happened. She wanted to make sure they understood she was trying to teach Mr. Damico a lesson and that she would handle his punishment. And also pay for a new fence."

"I can picture her doing that," I said.

Dad nodded. "She was as wise as she was kind."

I looked up at Mom. "How about you? Do you have a memory of G-Mags?"

Mom got up from her chair. "I have more than one, but this is my favorite. I'll be back in a minute to show you."

I gave Dad a puzzled look, but he offered no clue as to what Mom planned to show us.

When she returned, she was holding a tiny box with a green ribbon wrapped around it.

"What's in there?" I asked.

"You have to wait," Mom said. "It's part of the story." She sat next to me. "You know how I haven't been feeling well this summer?"

I nodded, hoping she wasn't really sick and that I wasn't wrong about the baby. I held my breath, waiting for her to continue.

"Well, one afternoon while you and Kevin were watching a movie, G-Mags gave me a cup of hot tea with grated ginger. She said it would make my stomach feel better."

"Is that what's in the box? Ginger?"

Mom shook her head. "No. It's something even better."

"C'mon," I said. "Hurry. Open the box." I gripped the seat of my chair and waited as she removed the lid. The tissue paper crinkled as Mom unfolded it. She looked up at me and said, "We'd been waiting to make sure everything is okay before we told anyone, but . . ." Then she pulled out the tiniest, cutest pair of sea green baby booties I'd ever seen and handed them to me.

"I knew it!" I said, feeling their softness against my palms.

"Knew what?" Mom said.

"I looked up your symptoms on the Internet and I thought you might be having a baby."

Mom and Dad broke into huge smiles. Dad said, "I told you she'd figure it out."

Relief and pride mingled inside me, and then I realized something. "Wait! Did you tell G-Mags that you were having a baby?"

"No," Mom said. "She figured it out not long after she met me, and she crocheted these booties for the baby. That's the type of woman she was. Just like your dad said: wise and kind."

I put the soft booties back inside the box and blinked a few times. So, that explained why G-Mags hadn't looked surprised when I told her Mom was pregnant. She'd known all along.

Mom folded the tissue paper over the booties and looked up at me. "It's your turn."

I took a deep breath and sifted through all the memories of G-Mags I'd stored in my brain. "There were so many fun times I had with her. But one thing I'll always remember is how interested she was in what everyone else had to say or do. I loved how excited she'd get when I'd show her my fossils. And how just yesterday she explained that they were nature's art. She made me look at my own artwork in a new way. Like what I was doing was important." My voice cracked. "And just like the impression of the fish on my fossil, G-Mags made an impression on my heart that will stay there forever."

Mom gave me a hug, and we all raised our share of the cannoli in a toast to G-Mags.

As the shell crunched in my mouth, I savored the taste. Knowing I would never have another one exactly like that, it was sweeter than ever.

After finishing the last of it, I bowed my head and whispered, "May she rest in peace."

CHAPTER 41

Two months later, I sat in the car with Kevin's birthday presents on my lap, tapping my foot to the music on Mom's favorite oldies radio station. I wasn't really listening to the words. I was too nervous about meeting Kevin's friends at his party.

He and I had seen each other lots of times since summer ended. The first time was the funeral. But I still hadn't met all his friends.

"You're awfully quiet," Mom said. "I thought you'd be happy to finally give Kevin this painting you've been working on for so long."

I smoothed my hand across the wrapping paper, which read *Happy Birthday* written in sand. "I hope he likes it."

"Of course he will."

As we pulled into the Damicos' driveway, I was nervous and excited at the same time.

I stepped out of the car and made sure I hadn't messed up the green ribbon on one of the gifts. I checked out my jeans and jacket to make sure everything was in place. Abbey had been right. The black velvet blazer was perfect with dark denim. It was a good thing I'd let her talk me into buying it at the mall. I'm still not into fashion as much as she is, but I know now there's an art to the things she's into. I can appreciate that.

And, once she explained that she'd stopped texting and e-mailing because she wasn't allowed to have her phone at summer camp—not because she didn't like me anymore—we were totally best friends again.

"Don't worry," Mom said. "You'll have a wonderful time with Kevin's friends."

I smiled up at her. How did she always know what I was thinking? Maybe there was such a thing as magic when it came to moms.

As we climbed the steps to the front door, a chill wind blew my hair across my face. I tucked the long strand behind my ear while Mom rang the bell.

I swallowed hard as the door opened. "Hey, everyone," Kevin said. "It's Haleigh."

A chorus of "Hey," sounded before everyone went back to what they were doing.

I held out the gifts. "Happy birthday."

Kevin looked at the wrapping paper and smiled.

"Open them later," I said. "After everyone leaves."

"Sure." He looked up at Mom and then at her protruding belly. "I heard it's a boy," he said.

Mom nodded. "Yes. And I hear that Michael is planning to give Haleigh some tips about having a little brother."

A voice came from around a corner. "Did someone mention my name?"

I'd met Michael at the funeral, but as soon as I looked into his face, it struck me even more how much he looked like a taller version of Kevin.

Michael put his hands on Kevin's shoulders. "If your brother's anything like this guy, Rule Number One: start watching *Star Wars* videos ASAP." We all laughed, and Mom left to join the adults in the kitchen.

I had a strong urge to ask Michael about his painting. When did he realize the portrait looked just like Kevin? Did he know the paints were magic?

I waited until we were alone together and asked him if he remembered the yellow box that G-Mags found in her closet.

He got a faraway look in his eyes. "I sure do," he said. "I was so bored that summer—all I wanted was someone to play with. Then G-Mags found those paints, and I did the portrait that ended up looking like Kevin." He scratched his head. "Of course, I didn't realize until almost four years later that it resembled him. It was the weirdest thing. I wondered whatever happened to those paints. Did G-Mags still have them?"

I nodded. "Yes, she gave them to me."

"That's great. What did you do with them?"

"Um, I painted a picture of my last day of summer."

"So, how did it turn out?"

I debated whether I should pour out my story. But all I said was, "Great."

Was that a twinkle in his eye that I spotted? I wasn't

sure. But as I smiled back at him, I felt a connection between us.

I never told Kevin about the paints either. Or what happened on our very last day together. He remembered only the first August twenty-sixth. And when I thought about telling him the truth, it sounded so crazy, I didn't believe it myself.

Even though Dad said a few scientists think time travel could be possible one day, if someone offered me a ride in a time machine back to August, I'd say, "No."

I didn't need to go back in time to save summer. I'd have it forever—in my painting.

The party went by quickly and I had a great time with Kevin's friends. Once they all left, Kevin pulled out the two gifts I'd brought. I held my breath. Would he like them? Or would the memories they brought make him sad?

He jiggled the first package and turned it over a couple of times. "Is it a book?"

I shook my head and smiled. "Just open it."

He ripped the paper off and held up the canvas. At first he was quiet. Then his eyes began to water.

A wave of regret came over me as I watched Kevin wipe his eyes with his fist. "It's amazing," he said. "It looks just like her."

"I hope so." I'd tried to capture everything about G-Mags: her kind face, her sparkling eyes, her love for family and friends. "I painted her in the kitchen—because that's how I'll always remember her."

"Me too." Kevin pointed to her hand, poised just above a pot. "What's that she's holding?"

"It's rosemary. For remembrance."

Kevin smiled and put the painting down.

"I hoped it wouldn't make you sad."

"It's okay," he said. "It's kind of a good sad. You know what I mean?"

"I'm not sure."

"Well, G-Mags is gone. But now I have this picture that reminds me of her and of how great the summer was and how you and I met and how we're all friends, and you're going to have a little brother."

I wiped my eyes and gestured for Kevin to open the smaller package.

He ripped the paper off to reveal the DVDs from Mr. Sidhu's store.

"Whoa! This is too much. You shouldn't have . . ."

"It's okay. A few weeks ago, we went down the shore and I sold a painting." I didn't tell Kevin who I sold it to. He'd never believe the eavesdropping man in the restaurant bought one of my abstract paintings.

"I always said you were a great artist." He examined the DVDs. "Now we can watch *The Day the Earth Stood Still* from the beginning." His eyes brightened and the corners of his mouth curled up. I knew what he was going to say before he said it: "*Klaatu barada nikto.*"

Hearing the words sent me back to G-Mags's kitchen.

"Are you okay?" Kevin said. "You looked like you were somewhere else for a second."

"I was just thinking about summer: the cottage, the cannolis . . ." I raised my eyebrows. "The cow suit. For a second I thought I could even smell rosemary."

"You did!" Kevin exclaimed. "My mom made ragout. She remembered how much you liked it."

I grabbed his hand and tugged him forward. "Well then, what are we waiting for? Let's get a *mooove* on."

ACKNOWLEDGMENTS

Like Haleigh's last day of summer, this novel had more do-overs than I can count. Fortunately, the following amazing people were there for me during the process.

My agent, Steven Chudney: You hung in there for all the revisions and never stopped believing. I can't thank you enough for your loyalty, persistence, and humor, and for finding the perfect home for this novel.

My editor, Fiona Simpson: You understood my vision perfectly and made this book the best it could be. I thank you for steering it through its various stages with so much care, for editing with such an astute eye, and, most of all, for teaching me to trust the reader.

Laura Lyn DiSiena and Pascal Campion: Together, the two of you created a cover more beautiful than I ever could have imagined. I am amazed and grateful for your time and talents.

Everyone at Aladdin: Thank you for all that you do behind the scenes, for welcoming me onto your team, and for working so hard to come up with a great new title.

Linda Adler and Debra Frank: Many thanks for

your encouragement on an earlier version of this novel and for your years of friendship. I wish we could go back and have a do-over of just one day in junior high, knowing what we know now.

Flora Doone, Debbie Reed Fischer, Alexandra Flinn, and Laurie Tadonnio: You cheered me on during various versions of this novel. Each of you, in your own unique way, contributed something invaluable, and I thank you for that.

Amy Linn and Lorin Oberweger: Your expert opinions made me aware of things I might never have noticed on my own. My characters and I are grateful.

Julie Arpin, Kathy Macdonald, and Gloria Rothstein: Your willingness along the way to read and critique so many versions and parts of this novel without ever complaining has meant everything to me. I am so lucky to have you as friends.

The Florida SCBWI, and, in particular, Linda Bernfeld: Your support has been invaluable to me as a writer, critiquer, and teacher. I thank you for believing in my work and my abilities.

James Lewis: If it weren't for your taking us to Atlantic City on our visits to New Jersey, this novel would have been a very different one, indeed. Many thanks for being our chauffeur and guide—even though I never hit the jackpot.

Nancy Knutson: A conversation about what type of book your school library needed gave me inspiration for parts of this book. Many thanks for that conversation and for your friendship.

Brett Kushner: This book wouldn't have been the same without those weird and wonderful conversations in car pool or your ubiquitous cow costume. Thank you for being so "amoosing."

My readers, especially those who have reached out to tell me how much my books have meant to them: A story isn't really finished until others read it and make it their own. You have my deep gratitude for "finishing" my books.

Blaise Koncsol: Your love and humor sustain me. Thank you for always helping me find the funny parts in life, and in my writing as well. I would not be the same person if I hadn't had you.

Siena Koncsol: If I'd put in an order for the perfect daughter for me, I couldn't have done better. How fortunate I am to have someone in my life who loves books as much as I do and who is willing to read everything I write. There are no words strong enough to tell you how much I appreciate you.

Stephen Koncsol: Thank you for supporting and encouraging my writing all these years and for telling me about how you burned down your neighbor's fence. While I'm not condoning such behavior, it was a perfect addition to the novel. If there were such things as do-overs, I'd do everything all over again with you.